EAT PREY AND *NO LOVE*

EAT PREY AND *NO LOVE*

TY MARSHALL

DEDICATION

"This book is dedicated to my beautiful wife Tiphony Marshall. Without her hard work, patience, unwavering love and support, none of this would be possible or as fun to do. And to the memories of my grandfather Nathaniel Holliman, my uncle Nate & my father-in-law Benjamin Rivera."

WORD FROM THE AUTHOR

"Every hustler dreams of the day he no longer has to risk his freedom to feed his family and I'm thankful to be afforded the opportunity to do just that. God has blessed me with the ability to use my mind and talent to re-invent my hustle. I look forward to this new journey with so much excitement and I invite the readers to join me for the ride. Let the story begin…" – Ty Marshall

PROLOGUE

Mr. Hill,
This letter is to inform you that we have decided to DENY
your request for an early release. You will be eligible for a
review of this decision in 6 months from the date above.
State Parole Board

Omar tossed the letter onto the bed beside him and laid back on his bunk. His dream of going home early had once again been shattered. He swore this time would be the one. In his mind he had met all the requirements asked of him by the board at his previous hearing. Their main issue was him staying out of trouble— something that hadn't come natural to him. Omar sought out trouble. It was all he had ever known. Since a child he had been in and out of the system starting with stints in JJC, followed by multiple trips to county jail. His latest brush with the law had landed him in state prison with a 1 to 3. He had done a little over a year and a half and had hoped to be granted an early release. His frustration was apparent to his cellmate, Rah, as he entered their cell.

"Dem maa'fuckas denied you huh?"

"Hell yeah," Omar said sitting up on his bed as he seen Rah step inside the cell. "And I did all da shit dey asked, dey playin' wit a nigga freedom."

"I feel you my G. You just gotta keep doin' whatchu been doin'. Keep the C.O.'s off ya back, stay away from dee'z fuck niggas and stay… in… the… library. You stay on them weights, but you need to build ya mind up too. Ya feel me?" Rah said schooling his younger celly.

O didn't fuck with too many niggas in the streets to begin with so keeping to himself behind the wall wasn't a problem. He had a few issues when he first touched down, but after showing he was nice with his hands and wasn't scared to get into it with anybody, inmates left him alone. He became cellmates with Rah after he cut his last celly with a razor across the cheek during a fight. He clicked with Rah immediately; he too was no stranger to the judicial system. He was currently serving his second stint in state prison. He was on his fourth year of a 7 to 15 sentence he had received for an assault with a deadly weapon charge. He would constantly try to drop jewels on Omar, recognizing that the youngster had plenty of street smarts. Rah would always kick it to him about the importance of having both. He would always say, "O, look at a nigga like Hov. That's why he's winning."

O sat on the bunk letting what Rah said soak in. "Yeah I feel you," he said, really meaning it for the first time. He was truly ready to go home and get back to the money. He knew that he would need a new hustle because he would be looking at a lot more time if he was to get arrested again. And for what? Little petty nickel and dime hustles that weren't worth the time they came with.

"Anyway, I'm 'bout to hit da dance floor. I gotta visit. My wifey and daughter here," Rah said with a smile stretched across his face as he grabbed the shirt off the top bunk.

"Dats what's up," O said happy for his friend, but a little sad for himself. He hadn't had a visit his whole bid and wasn't expecting one. Besides messing with a few females here and there, he never stayed still long enough to grow roots. He was a hustler and went where ever the money was. It was all he knew and it was what he did best. It was the mentality his drug addicted mother had forced upon him at an early age by sending him out into the streets to find ways to support her drug habit. At 10 years old he was already the man of the house. Snatching pocketbooks, robbing old ladies and selling drugs just to make sure the lights stayed on and his mother could get her fix and wouldn't get dope sick.

He watched as Rah exited the cell then reached for the deck of cards on the desk, flipping the top card over revealing a 10 of diamonds. O got down on the floor of the cell and started doing pushups. "1...2...3...4..."

* * *

Rah's eyes scanned the rec room looking for his cellmate. He was in a good mood after seeing his wife and daughter. His wife always came, but his daughter was now in college so she didn't get to visit him as much anymore. He really cherished the times when he got to see her. He spotted O sitting near the front of the room watching TV. Rah made his way over to where he was.

"Look at you nigga. You slipping." Rah said, trying to catch O off his square.

"Never that my G," O said as he moved his shirt a little showing his friend the ox he was holding in his hand. "I ain't worried about none of dee'z niggas in here."

Rah shook his head and laughed. He knew O was never off and wouldn't hesitate to use his weapon if given the chance. No matter how many jewels he shared with him, he knew he was still a live wire at heart.

"Come on O, get a game of chess wit me," Rah said tapping O. Nobody could fuck with Rah on the chess board. He was an OG and would school niggas on a daily.

The two men sat at the table locked in an intense game. Omar had been a novice chess player entering jail. But after spending the last year playing against Rah, he had become a great player. He enjoyed the mental part of the game, the need to be able to see things before they happen. He didn't know it, but Rah was teaching him life lessons while they were playing, showing him the need to be able to think 2 or 3 moves ahead. Teaching him how to remain calm and make smart decisions. O didn't know it yet, but he would need to rely heavily on those lessons if he was to make it out in the world and avoid coming back through the jail's revolving doors. He was in deep thought on his next move when Rah broke his concentration and directed his attention towards the TV.

"There goes your boy," Rah said pointing at the screen.

O lifted his head to see who Rah was talking about. Then he saw his favorite rapper, Jay-Z, on the screen on the red carpet with his wife at one of those black tie galas with the $30,000 dinner seats.

"Yeah he doin' it," O said calmly, admiring the moves the rapper was making.

"Yeah he is…. street smarts…book smarts." Rah said, trying to drive his point home from their earlier discussion.

Omar vaguely heard his last statement though. Something else on the TV had caught his attention. He stared at the screen in amazement. He couldn't believe his eyes.

CHAPTER ONE

Two Years Later

Bryce began to feel tired. It had been a long week full of excitement. Being the only child of a wealthy real estate developer sure had its perk: private schooling, private jets, private island vacations and countless amounts of homes. This particular week had been special not only because the house his parents owned in St. Thomas was his favorite of all, but because his best friend, Tremaine, had been brought along on this family vacation. Bryce and Tremaine met when Bryce's father made him tag along to one of his many community events in Atlanta, at a local home for abandoned children and children born to drug addicts. Tremaine was one of the latter, but he and Bryce had so much in common, despite their very different circumstances in life, and became fast friends. They both enjoyed watching and playing sports— basketball being their favorite, collecting trading cards, and they both were very smart young men. Mrs. Edwards, who wasn't able to have any more children after giving birth to Bryce, had really taken to Tremaine like a second son over the past few months, even trying to convince her husband to adopt him. She was always so amazed at how much the two 12 year old boys resembled each other and could actually pass for maybe not twins, but definitely brothers. This trip not only marked the first time Tremaine had been on a plane, but had been outside the state of Georgia and he had enjoyed every minute of it, especially the luxuries of being on a private jet. He was scared to death before the plane took off for the flight, but now was enjoying the flight back like a seasoned pro. Bryce's father told the boys before they boarded the plane for the flight home that he had one more surprise for them once they reached Atlanta. No matter how hard they tried to get him to spill the beans he wouldn't crack. Bryce decided he had enough of trying about five minutes into the plane ride. He let the music blasting in his headphones drown out any noise from the outside world. After watching Tre's failed attempts for another ten minutes or so, Bryce eventually removed his headphones. "He's not gonna tell us," he informed his best friend while passing him the CD player. "If you want to listen to something else there are more CDs in my backpack and the new SLAM magazine is in there too."

"Oh Ok." Tre replied finally realizing Mr. Edwards wasn't going to crack no matter what he did. He grabbed the CD player, *stuck his arms through the straps of the backpack so that it rested on his chest and began looking through the assortment of CDs.*

Bryce looked out the window one last time at the beautiful blue water just as the sun began to disappear and thought to himself how life couldn't be much better than it was at this very moment, then he leaned his seat back and gave in to his heavy eyelids. He had only been sleep for what felt like twenty minutes or so when he heard a loud noise that shook the plane and woke him. He could smell something burning and when he opened his eyes he could see smoke slowly beginning to fill the cabin of the plane. His mother began to panic and he could see all those fears Tremaine had about flying instantly return. His father remained calm as he got up out his seat and walked to the cockpit to see exactly what was going on. Bryce could hear the pilot tell his father that there was a problem. One of the plane's engines had caught on fire and they needed to land immediately. Over the Atlantic with no land in sight, their plane was now freefalling fast. Mr. Edwards returned to his seat and yelled for everyone to buckle their safety belts and brace themselves for impact....

* * *

Bryce's alarm clock went off causing him to sit up in his bed, happy to be awakened from his recurring nightmare. Almost every night for the past seventeen years, Bryce had been reliving the fatal plane crash that claimed the lives of his parents and best friend. Despite the tragedy, he managed to do pretty well for himself. He graduated high school a year early and enrolled at Morehouse. He excelled very well, graduating at the top of his class before taking over as the Chairman and CEO of Edwards Developments Inc, the company started by his father, and left to him in the will. In an article done on him by Black Enterprise Magazine, it was speculated that he was worth an estimated 435 million dollars and he was still a few months away from his 29th birthday. He had truly picked up where his father left off. He initially concentrated on low to middle income rental housing, revitalizing apartment complexes in and around the city of Atlanta, raising their occupancy rate then flipping them for a profit. He eventually began to expand outside of the state and then on to high end residential properties and hotels. It wouldn't be long before his company was listed on the New York Stock Exchange which would make him, as well as a few of its shareholders billionaires, something he hoped to do before he turned 35. Bryce had truly inherited his father's business savvy along with his charitable spirit and today was no different. It was his annual "Back to School" giveaway and concert. Every kid would receive a brand new book bag stuffed with everything they would need for the new school year. Plus he was giving away laptops, tablets, and two one thousand dollar shopping sprees. There would be free food and drinks for all, plus a performance by a surprise invited guest and some local acts.

Bryce noticed a note sitting on the pillow on the

opposite side of his California King bed so he reached and grabbed it.

Had fun last night. Sorry I had to run. I didn't want to wake you. See you later.

The note has been kissed by lipstick worn lips.

Bryce smiled as thoughts of last night ran through his mind. With no wife or kids, he was one of the most eligible bachelors on the market and he definitely enjoyed his bachelor lifestyle.

He hopped out of bed and made his way into the master bathroom of his penthouse apartment in Buckhead. He dropped his boxers, stepped inside the oversized shower, and turned it on. He stood there enjoying the hot water shooting out of the walls hitting his body from all directions, allowing it to wake him up fully before washing his body. When finished he grabbed a towel and wrapped it around his waist while walking over to the mirror. Standing nearly 6'1, Bryce was built like a world class athlete. His body looked like a young Roy Jones Jr. His caramel skin was flawless and his smile matched his bank account. The low taper with thick waves he sported always seemed as if it had just been cut. With his skin still wet he rubbed some shaving gel on his face, grabbed his razor and began removing any hairs that had popped up around his neatly trimmed goatee overnight. He finished up and then began brushing his teeth when he heard one of his phones ring a few times then stop

TY MARSHALL

in the bedroom. He finished brushing his pearly whites before heading back into the bedroom to see who had made the missed call. Picking his phone up he saw that he had actually missed three calls, all from the same name and number. He put the phone down and made his way into his walk-in closet and tried to decide what to wear. He eventually decided on a black Polo V-neck t-shirt, black cargo shorts, and the Lebron 9 Miami Nights. He put on a pair of princess cut diamond earrings, snapped his black Breitling Supersport on his wrist, grabbed a pair of shades and headed for the door to start his day. When he got downstairs to the parking garage he couldn't decide which vehicle to drive, but eventually chose his white Bentley Mulsanne over his Range Rover. As the car started up, 2 Chainz began playing out of the speakers. He rolled his windows down and pulled out of the underground parking garage headed for Centennial Park.

The event was about to start when he pulled up and parked, then made his way over towards the mass amount of people that had shown up. The big turnout was exactly what he had hoped for. Helping those that were less fortunate was something that really put a smile on his face. That smile quickly disappeared when he saw a familiar face making its way through the crowd stalking towards him. He could always tell when Mia, his on again off again girlfriend, was mad and he knew exactly what to do to get her that way.

17

Today he didn't know her exact reason. Maybe it was the honey brown beauty with the Melyssa Ford body she saw him having lunch with a few days ago or maybe it had something to do with the three missed calls from earlier. Either way he knew he was about to find out.

"So you're not answering my calls now?" she barked stepping in front of him.

"I don't know what you're talking about," he said nonchalantly.

"Bryce don't play with me. I was just trying to make sure you would be on time. This event is very important to these kids."

"Ok, well I'm here and as you can see I'm on time, bye," he said sarcastically as he tried to step around her.

"Oh so we're playing that game now?" Mia said impeding him by putting her hand on his chest.

"Haven't we been?" Bryce shot back, removing her hand and walking away leaving her standing there.

Bryce and Mia had a long standing relationship. They were high school friends turned college sweethearts. Mia Armstrong graduated from Spelman and had become a very accomplished criminal lawyer at one of the top firms in the city of Atlanta, where she was on the fast track to becoming a partner. They dated off and on after college, but had become very serious the past year after always being close friends. That was until a few months ago when Mia decided she didn't want to continue their relationship after he told her he wasn't ready to get married. Bryce tried for weeks to talk to her, but Mia refused to see him or take his calls. Eventually getting the message, Bryce returned to the dating scene. They hadn't seen each other until they bumped into one another a few days ago, but he knew she would be here. Mia never missed this event. Just like him she grew up privileged and enjoyed being able to help and give back.

As Bryce made his way towards the stage he couldn't help but to think about his quick encounter with Mia. Not so much the friction that was going on between them, but how good she looked with her new haircut. She chopped off her long flowing locks and was now rocking a Meagan Good short hairstyle that really fit her beautiful face and brought out her light colored eyes. Not every woman could pull off such a drastic switch. Mia not only pulled it off but she was killing it. Bryce stepped on the stage and quickly changed gears back to the reason everyone came out.

"Hello everybody, I'd like to thank each and every one of you for coming out. It's so good to see all the parents and children out here on this beautiful afternoon. As most of you may know my name is Bryce Edwards. I was born and raised right here in Atlanta and every chance I get I try to give back to this city and to the people of this city that gave so much to me. Many of you know I do this event every year for the kids and every year I try to make it bigger and better than the year before. So hopefully I was able to do that. But I'm not going talk everyone's head off. I'm going to turn it over to the host for this afternoon's festivities, Mr. Ryan Cameron. Enjoy yourselves!" he said as he handed the microphone over to the host and walked off the stage.

Stepping off the stage Erica, the honey brown beauty from lunch or more recently the author of the letter on his pillow this morning, was waiting for him with a microphone and a camera crew. Far removed from the sex kitten she was the night before she was now doing her day job, being the lead reporter for Channel 2 news.

"So Mr. Edwards how does it feel to see such a huge turnout today?" she asked.

"It feels good. There is no better feeling than being able to help somebody."

"Being the son of Gabriel Edwards and with your father being so active in the community, are events like this your way of honoring his memory?"

"Well not just with the events, but I try to honor his memory by the way I live my life period. Giving back and uplifting those who are less fortunate was definitely a passion of my father's and I think that is something I inherited. It's all about working hard, staying focused, and not forgetting about the people who aren't as blessed as you." Bryce stated into the camera with a smile.

"Times being the way they are right now, with so many

people out of work, this is something that is needed." Erica expressed to him.

"I'm just trying to do my part. It's small but it's just one less thing these parents have to worry about. Every little bit helps."

"It sure does Mr. Edwards. Well thanks for your time. It's been a pleasure talking to you."

"The pleasure was all mine," he charmingly flirted.

"I'm Erica West reporting live from Centennial Park for Channel 2 news. Now back to you guys in the studio."

With the cameras now off and the camera crew gone to get shots of the festivities, Erica was able to comment on his camera flirting.

"So, the pleasure was all yours huh? You just couldn't help yourself?"

"You handled it good. You didn't choke or anything you just kept going," he said.

"That's because I'm a professional."

"Ok, are we talking 'bout the interview or last night?" Bryce said with a grin on his face.

"Both nasty!" Erica gushed while pushing him in the chest.

"Oh I'm nasty now? You wasn't saying that last night," Bryce bragged.

"Was too! Last night it was a compliment though," she said causing them to both laugh. "Anyway, what's all that 'It's small, I'm just doing my part' talk? Rumor has it you spent close to a million dollars on this event."

"What is that some of your investigative journalism?" he facetiously asked. "Don't believe everything you hear. Plus it's all for a good cause."

"Yeah, but that's still a lot of money Bryce."

"I know right. At this rate I'll only be able to do this for what? 400 more years?" Bryce said showing his sardonic wit.

"Whatever. Well let me get back to work before people start thinking something," she said as she smiled and walked away.

"Let em' think it," Bryce replied smiling back.

He stood there watching the sexy reporter strut away. Turning to walk away he spotted Mia, who was standing about 15 feet away and had been watching them the whole time. When they made eye contact she just shook her head in disgust then turned and stormed away towards the group of kids lining up to meet and take pictures with some NBA stars. Bryce just laughed to himself. That was the typical Mia. She had broken it off with him, refused to talk to him for weeks, and now she was acting as if he had done something to her. She was a Taurus and true to form she was one stubborn woman. He made his way around to the front of the stage where he was greeting some of the kids and their parents who just wanted to say thanks for all that he's done.

While waiting at the beverage stand for an Arnold

Palmer, Bryce looked around at all the smiles on everyone's face and thought to himself how truly blessed he was to be in a position to not only to put their smiles there, but to witness them. He wasn't like other rich people who donated money or put their names on fundraisers but never actually showed up to the events. Ever since the plane crash he felt like he was living on borrowed time and he was determined to make the best of it and do the best with it. That was why he put 100% into everything he did. That was why he wasn't ready to marry Mia. He knew he wasn't ready to give her the 100% of him he felt she deserved.

He was snapped out of his deep thought by a tap on the shoulder from Andre Daye, the Director of Operations at Edwards Hall. Edward Hall was the home once frequented by Bryce and his father but now owned by Bryce. He renamed the place and recently put Andre in charge; mainly because he was one of the success stories. He had lived in the home as a youth until he was adopted and went to college and now he was back running the place. Bryce remembered him from when he used to go visit Tremaine and thought he would be an inspiration to the kids there.

"Whassup Bryce. This is really a good thing you got going on here for the kids."

"I know what you mean. I remember when your dad used to do stuff like this for us at the home. It didn't matter what bad thing was going on in my life at that time. When your dad would come over all that went out the window and we were able to just have fun, like normal kids," Andre acknowledged.

"Speaking of Edwards Hall, how's everything going so far?" Bryce inquired.

"Everything is good. It feels good to be back there. I see a lot of myself in these kids and I just want to do everything in my power to give them the chance to be successful."

"That's the reason I put you in charge. So are they ready for the Six Flags trip?"

"Yeah they are. I didn't even know about it. They told me."

"Ha-ha, that's my fault I should have told you. I do it every year right before they go back to school. It allows them to get that last little bit of summer energy out of their system," Bryce informed him.

"Yeah that's smart."

"But I'll come by Tuesday to fill you in on everything. I'm 'bout to go back over by the stage." Bryce said, hearing Ryan Cameron announcing the surprise guest, Drake, as the next artist to perform.

After the show Bryce came back out on stage to thank everyone for coming and everyone who had something to do with the event. Then he told all the workers and volunteers who had helped about a surprise "Thank you" dinner he had planned for them. Everyone clapped and cheered as he walked off the stage.

CHAPTER TWO

Bryce pulled his black on black Ferrari F12 into the parking garage underneath the high rise that read The Edwards Building atop of it, right in the heart of midtown Atlanta. He loved this car more than any of his many others. The newspapers and magazines had labeled him the black Bruce Wayne due to his tragic past and lavish lifestyle; he referred to it as the Bat Mobile. His Monday's were usually very hectic so he always came in a little earlier than usual to get a jump start. It was something he recommended to his employees but didn't require because he loved to see who would take the initiative to do it. He parked in his reserved spot and stepped out dressed in a grey suit, white dress shirt, with a lavender colored tie with his gold Rolex on his wrist. His hair and goatee were freshly trimmed, waves were spinning, and he smelled good as usual. When the elevator opened up on the 44th floor he was greeted by the company name embedded on the wall in the lobby area of the gigantic office. He spoke to the secretary and continued down the hallway, ducking his head into a couple offices to speak to some of his employees as he passed by. His administrative assistant, Yolanda, was already at her desk hard at work once he reached his part of the office.

"Good morning Yolanda."

"Good morning Mr. Edwards," she said looking up seeing her boss. "How was your weekend?"

"Good and yours? How'd everything work out with your daughter?" he asked.

"She is doing much better. I think she just had a little 24 hour bug."

"Oh ok, that's good to hear."

"I put some papers on your desk and you have a few callback messages already."

"Ok, thanks."

He walked into his office and closed the door behind him. With the view from his office he could see the Georgia Dome, Phillips Arena, and the CNN building. He sat his briefcase down next to his desk, removed his suit jacket, placed it on the back of the chair, and sat down. He found the remote on the desk and pressed power. It turned on the 3 flat screens across the room in the lounge area of the office.

The 3 televisions stayed locked on the same 3 channels: CNN, CNBC, and ESPN. He touched the keyboard, turning on the computer and began flipping through the paperwork Yolanda had left on his desk. Bryce noticed that one of the missed messages had been from Natasha Cozier, an international designer he wanted to hire to design his newest project for a luxury hotel & residence called The Phoenix. He immediately put on his earpiece and told Yolanda to get the designer on the phone.

Once the two were connected they exchanged admiration for one another's work and decided to meet next week to discuss the possibilities of working with each other. Bryce told his assistant to take care of all the arrangements. She was to have his private jet pick the designer up and book dinner reservations for their meeting.

Bryce was just about to wrap up another one of his early morning phone meetings when there was a knock on his door before it opened and Marcus stuck his head in. Bryce waved for him to come in and continued with his phone conversation. Once he was done he hung up and turned his attention to his friend sitting on one of the couches in the lounge area watching SportsCenter.

Marcus Gilyard was Bryce's college roommate. He was also a top exec at EDI. When Bryce took over the company straight out of college, he brought his best friend along with him. Marcus was the closest thing Bryce had to a brother since Tremaine. They did everything together from sporting events and traveling to enjoying the company of many different women. If Bryce was Batman then Marcus was truly Robin.

"What's good? I missed you this weekend at the event for the kids. What happened?" Bryce asked.

"I thought I told you I wasn't gonna be able to make it. I had to fly to Cali. It was shawty I been telling you about birthday weekend," Marcus replied.

"I do remember you saying something about that. What did ya'll do?"

"Vegas, nothing crazy just did a lil' gambling."

"You've been flying out to Cali a lot lately. You and ol' girl getting serious or something? You haven't even introduced her to your boy yet and you bout to wife that up."

"Nah nothing like that, just like kicking it with her plus the head is crazy."

"Yeah? I am not mad at that. She has any friends?" Bryce asked causing them to both laugh.

"How'd the event go?" Marcus asked.

"Everything as far as the kids was fine. It was just me who had a lil' trouble," Bryce informed him.

"What you mean?" Marcus asked with his interest now peaked.

"You know I fucked Erica West right?" Bryce bragged.

"The bad ass news reporter bitch? When?"

"Friday night. Peep this, Channel 2 sent her to cover the event so after I did an interview with her and the cameras went off, me and her stood there flirting back and forth talking shit. She walked away and as I turned around, guess who was standing right there listening to the whole thing?... Mia."

"Wait, Mia was there? She showed up?" a confused Marcus questioned.

"Yes nigga, looking good too."

"Oh shit!"

"Oh shit is right," Bryce continued. "She looked at me like she wanted to kill me. But I'm like why she mad? She the one who broke it off with me."

"Yeah after you told her you didn't want to marry her," Marcus reminded him.

"I never said that. I said I wasn't ready to get married."

"Same thing," Marcus declared.

Just then Bryce's assistant Yolanda buzzed in. "Mr. Edwards, there's a Kendrick Price here to see you."

"Ok, send him in," Bryce said to her snapping back into business mode. "Yo, let me take this meeting. We'll continue this later. Go grab lunch or something," he said as he turned to Marcus.

"Alright, I need to get back to work anyway," Marcus replied.

"Yeah I was just thinking the same thing," Bryce jokingly

said.

Kendrick was one of the many kids Bryce was paying for to go to college. He was a junior at the University of South Carolina with a major in International Business. Out of all the kids Bryce helped he was definitely one of his favorites. He would always come by and volunteer at Edwards Hall when he was home from school and was a straight A student. Bryce told him once he graduated from college he had a job waiting for him. Kendrick opened the door and stepped into the office just as Marcus was leaving.

"Hey, what's good Kendrick? Come in and have a seat. You want something to drink?" Bryce greeted him.

"No, I'm fine Mr. Edwards but thanks anyway though," he replied.

"Ok, so what do I owe the pleasure of this visit? Everything is ok, right?" Bryce asked seeing the look on the young man's face.

"Well," the young man said reluctantly. "I'm having a few problems at home."

"What kind of problems?"

"Well my mom lost her job and she has fallen behind on some of the bills. They just put an eviction notice on our door and our lights have been out for two days now. I'm about to go back to school where all my needs are taken care of, but I don't want to leave her, my sister and nephew like that," Kendrick said all in one breath.

"Kendrick, why are you just now coming to me with this?" Bryce said as he looked at him in shock.

"I know you always told me if I needed anything just ask, but you already have done so much for me. I didn't want to bother you. I just don't know what else to do."

"Say no more, I will take care of everything," Bryce said jumping up from his seat and grabbing his suit jacket.

With his busy day finally coming to an end, Bryce was ready to get out and enjoy himself. He and Marcus planned to meet up later at the comedy club. With the show still a few hours away Bryce had some time to kill. Making it to his apartment just in time to catch the 6 o'clock SportsCenter and fixing himself a drink from his fully stocked bar seemed like the perfect way to do just that.

Pulling his white Range Rover into the parking lot of the comedy club, he spotted Marcus's 745 BMW and parked next to him. When they got inside they grabbed a seat at a table, ordered a couple of drinks and began checking out the scene. Atlanta nightlife was always exciting because Atlanta had some of the finest women on the planet. Light, dark, short, tall, slim or thick— if God made it, Atlanta had it. The two of them were enjoying the scenery and working on their second round of drinks, when Marcus spotted Mia and a few of her girlfriends entering the club. They passed right in front of their table but Mia pretended not to see them.

Marcus really got a kick out of the way Mia was treating Bryce. "Mia is cold-blooded, she really hates you bruh," he teased his friend.

"She just putting on a show. Mia knows how I feel about her."

"Yeah, I don't really think the feeling is mutual right now," Marcus continued joking, amusing himself.

"Whatever, she still loves me. If she didn't she would have spoken."

"Huh?" a confused Marcus stopped laughing and asked.

"If she didn't love me she would have spoken because it wouldn't have been a big deal seeing me. But since she didn't, it's obvious she still cares."

As Mia and her two friends, Kim and Latrice, sat waiting for the waitress to return with their drinks, Latrice couldn't help herself or her big mouth.

"Look at Bryce trifling ass sitting over there soaking up all the attention from these thirsty hoes up in here. He get a kick out of all these women in Atlanta wanting his ass. Let one of them get dey claws in him, they gonna take em' for everything he got," the bronze color, slim but curvy loud mouth said.

"I'm not worried about Bryce. He made his choice and I've made mine. Life goes on. I came out to have a good time, not talk about my ex," Mia declared.

"Whatever, you know you still love Bryce," Kim, the

thick Lisa Raye lookalike, with long curly hair said.

"Love, yes but in love? Not anymore. Plus he's moved on so why shouldn't I?" Mia quipped.

"What you mean he's moved on?" Kim asked.

"Erica West."

"The bitch from the news? Oh hell no, he couldn't do better than that?" Latrice blurted out.

"Last week I bumped into them having lunch at FAB, then I caught them flirting at the event for the kids on Saturday."

"Well Mia, you did avoid him for almost 2 months. What was he supposed to do, sit at home and pray?" Kim asked.

"He didn't want to marry me. How long am I supposed to play house with him? I'm too old for that Kim. Whose side are you on anyway?"

"I'm on your side of course. I'm just saying you can't make a man marry you if he's not ready. You should be happy he was honest with you," Kim enlightened her friend.

"Whatever Oprah," Latrice interrupted. "All I know is if he loved her...he would have put a ring on it. He just wanna stay single so he can run around with that piece of shit Marcus, chasing their dicks," Latrice seethed.

"Shut up Latrice. You just mad because you slept with Marcus and he never called you again," Kim reminded her.

"Fuck Marcus, I didn't call his ass back neither," she said as the lights dimmed for the show to start.

* * *

Bryce and Marcus stood by their cars in the parking lot talking, as people spilled out the club, when they spotted Mia and her friends walking towards her car. Bryce told Marcus he would talk to him later and immediately jumped in his Range and raced over to where the three women were walking. As he approached he slowed to a creep and rolled his window down.

"Ya'll need a ride to ya'll car?" he asked.

The three women just ignored him and kept walking. So he asked again; this time Kim answered him.

"Hey Bryce, how you doing? No we're okay but thanks anyway," she said.

"How 'bout you Mia? You need a ride?" he asked, but still she ignored him and just kept on walking. "Mia!" he shouted. "Mia, I know you hear me. Can I just talk to you for a second? Can you just stop walking for a second and talk to me?" he pleaded.

"Bryce she ain't got nothing to say to you. So save yourself the embarrassment," Latrice stated sarcastically.

"Mia," he said once again.

"What Bryce? What do you want? What can you possibly have to say that I would want to hear?" Mia finally said.

"Can I just get five minutes?" he asked.

"You got two."

He put his hazard lights on, stopped in the middle of the street and jumped out to talk to her.

"Listen Mia I know things didn't end between us the right way or at least the way I would have liked, but I would love to have a chance to explain myself to you. But right here is not the proper place to have this conversation. So is it possible we can meet up and talk? You know without the audience," he said looking directly at Latrice.

"Why should I meet up with you Bryce? I tried to talk to you on Saturday and you tried to play me for your little news reporter hoe." Mia said getting her shot in.

"Nah Mia it's not even like that. I know that was the wrong way to handle it, and I'm sorry, but I do think we should talk," Bryce stated smoothly trying to turn on the charm.

"Ok well call my office and my secretary will tell you what day I have free for you to come by so we can talk," she said, shooting down his attempt at charming her.

"Come to your office? Call your office?" he said in disbelief.

"Do you wanna meet and talk or not?" she said point blank.

"Ok, ok your office it is," he said as he laughed to himself.

Bryce got back in his truck as Mia and her friends walked away. He drove to his penthouse apartment in silence thinking about all the things he needed to say to Mia when they met up, some of which he didn't know how she would take.

CHAPTER THREE

Bryce couldn't wait to tell Tremaine the good news. He almost jumped out his father's car before he could finish parking. He ran up the steps into the building, passing the front desk without even signing in and went looking for his friend. He found his friend in the activity room in the middle of a game of jacks. When Tremaine saw Bryce race in he stopped playing right in the middle of the game and walked over to meet him halfway. He could see the excitement on Bryce's face and was anxious to find out what it was for.

"What's up Bryce? What you so hype about?" he asked.

"They said yes!" Bryce said.

"They who? And said yes to what?" a confused Tremaine asked.

"My parents! They said yes you can go on vacation with us

next week."

"Fo'real?" he said in disbelief.

"Yes for real Tremaine," Mr. Edwards said as he walked up on the two friends. "My wife and I would love for you to accompany us on vacation; hopefully this could be the first of many."

"Aww man, Mr. Edwards thanks so much I can't wait."

"Yeah me neither, we're gonna have so much fun," Bryce said.

"Well ok, I'm gonna leave you boys to talk about it some more. I have to go in the office and finish filling out some paperwork so Tremaine is able to go with us," Mr. Edwards said.

"Ok, thanks again Mr. Edwards," Tremaine said with a big smile on his face.

"Yeah thanks dad," Bryce said as his dad turned to walk away...

* * *

Bryce opened his eyes and began staring at the ceiling. It didn't matter how many times he had that dream or where it started it always ended the same way. That was his reality, one that he still hadn't fully come to grips with. He often questioned himself about what he could have done differently. Maybe he could have pretended to be sick and the trip might have been cancelled or postponed. That most likely wouldn't have been the case, but he still couldn't help wonder what if. He rolled over and grabbed his phone that he used only for business and began scrolling through emails. With no meetings today, he really had no reason to go into the office; that didn't mean he was able to relax though. He had to drive out to Henry County to check on a housing community he was developing. He also had to drop by Edwards Hall and meet with his event planner to start discussing plans for his birthday that was just a few weeks away. He put his phone back on the nightstand and grabbed his other phone next to it. He scrolled down his contacts until he got to the number for Mia's office and pressed talk. The phone rung twice before it was picked up on the other end.

"Hamilton & Associates, Mia Armstrong's office— this is Angela speaking how may I help you?"

"Hello Angela this is Bryce. Mia should be expecting my call."

"Hello Mr. Edwards, Ms. Armstrong is actually in a meeting right now. Would you like to leave a message for her?"

"No, I'll call back. Thank you," he said before hanging up.

Angela got up from her desk and walked over to the open door to Mia's office and knocked.

"Come in Angie," Mia said.

"Bryce just called," Angela said as she entered the room.

"Did you tell him I was in a meeting?"

"Yes, just like you told me."

"Thank you."

Mia sat at her desk thinking long and hard about what it was that she wanted to do. On one hand she wanted to hear him out because she still loved him very much and wanted nothing more than to be with him. But she knew he needed to grow up and she wasn't sure if he was ready to, but even worst she didn't know if she could wait around for him. Maybe it was time to move on and go their separate ways for good. She was brought out of her daydream state by another knock at her office door. It was Christion Bradshaw, the firm's sexy new addition. He was originally from Harlem, graduated from NYU and worked for one of the best law firms in New York City before recently relocating to Atlanta to be closer to his ailing grandmother.

"Good morning Ms. Armstrong," he said as he stood at her door.

"Good morning Mr. Bradshaw," she said as she looked up and seen him.

"Did I interrupt something? You looked like you were in deep thought. I could comeback," Christion said noticing the look on her face.

"Oh no, not all. Come in, is there something I can help you with?"

"Actually there is," he said as he stepped all the way in her office. "I'm looking for something to eat."

Mia paused before answering, allowing her mind to

think nasty thoughts with the words her super sexy co-worker had just spoken.

"Come again," she said, no pun intended.

"I'm starving, and I'm tired of fast food. Can you pleeeease help me?" he said in desperation, causing Mia to burst into laughter. "So you just gonna laugh at me," he said with a smirk on his face.

"Yes," she said laughing harder. "Because you still haven't learned your way around yet and you've been here almost a month."

"I know, I know but are you gonna help me?" he asked again.

"Ok, I got you," she said as she tried to stop laughing. "I'm sorry, that's just the best laugh I've had in weeks."

"Well I'm glad I can be of some assistance," he said as he continued to flash his pearly whites.

"I'll have Angela put a list together for you and I'll have her email it to you with names and addresses. You do know how to use your navigation system right?"

"Oh you really got jokes huh?" he said.

"I'm just checking."

"Ok thanks Ms. Armstrong," he said as he turned to walk out of her office.

"Mia," she said causing him to stop.

"Huh?" he said as he turned back around.

"Mia, my name is Mia. It's ok for you to call me Mia."

"Oh I know your name; I was just waiting until you gave me permission to use it. I've never been the one to assume things especially when it comes to a woman," he said charmingly, then flashed that smile again before exiting her office.

* * *

Mia pulled her smoke grey 645 BMW into the parking garage next to the courthouse and parked. Despite the troubles in her personal life, her professional life was blossoming. She was one of the best up and coming criminal attorneys in the state and she was in high demand. As she stared back at herself through her rearview mirror the situation with Bryce was weighing heavy on her heart and mind. But she was right in the middle of one of the biggest trials of her career and refused to let it affect her performance. Mia was defending a 17 year old high school football player accused of murdering a local drug dealer in what was explained as a drug deal gone wrong. Mia had taken the case for free and from the beginning she was convinced that it was a case of mistaken identity. Today she was presenting the evidence that would prove it. She opened her car door and stepped out dressed in a black D&G business skirt suit with matching D&G high heel shoes. She grabbed her briefcase out of the backseat, closed the door and confidently strutted into the building.

* * *

Bryce walked through the door of Gladys Knight's Chicken & Waffles and immediately spotted Marcus and Eva, his event planner, sitting at one of the tables towards the back of the restaurant. When Eva saw Bryce she stood to greet him with a hug and kiss on the cheek. They had known each other for almost 13 years and besides being his event planner, Eva was Bryce's best female friend. He had given her the seed money for her company after she graduated from FAMU and now she was the go to person in Atlanta for all the record execs, entertainers, and athletes who wanted to have an event in the city. She did a great job for all her clients, but she always went the extra mile for Bryce. So when she called him telling him she had some ideas about his birthday he couldn't wait to hear what she had come up with.

"Hey bighead," she said as she hugged him.

"What's up Pucci," he said as he smiled and hugged her back.

"Wow, you just took it back. I haven't been called that since..."

"Your freshman year of high school— when your mom brought you up to the school so you could fight..."

"Niecey Williams!" she said as she remembered that exact event.

"Yup," he said as he began to laugh. "Man you whipped

that girl's ass. Whatever happened to her?"

"Ok, ok enough of the memory lane trip. I'm hungry, can we order now?" Marcus said interrupting their reminiscing session.

When they finished ordering their food and drinks, Bryce continued his conversation with Eva. "So what's been going on in the world of Eva?'

"Same old, same old just working hard trying to build this company up. I've been trying to establish contacts outside of Atlanta. You know New York, Miami, LA so I can start doing events in those cities as well," she said.

"Well you already know anything I can do to help I'm here."

"Yeah me too," Marcus said as he began flirting.

"Marcus please, don't you even start with your shit," she said as she quickly shot him down as usual.

"Why you always so mean to me Eva. A nigga ain't even say too much of nothing and you already shutting me down."

"Because….. how many times I got to tell you no before you get it?"

"How many times have you told me?" he questioned.

"At least a million," she snapped.

"Ok so you gonna have to tell me at least a million more before I give up, cuz I ain't no quitter," he said causing them all to burst out laughing.

"So what's going on with you and ol' boy? He can't use

some of that big time NBA star power to help his fiancé'?" Bryce said sarcastically.

"Yeah he could but just like I am with you, I won't allow him to. This is my company and I want to do it on my own. I don't want anybody to be able to say I owe my success to anything besides my hard work. That's why I insisted on paying you back your original investment. I don't want people saying I did it because of my wealthy best friend or my NBA husband," she quickly checked Bryce.

"Yeah speaking of which, when is this wedding?" Bryce said being sarcastic again.

"See here we go. What about you and Mia? How's that going?" she said quickly turning the tables.

"Oh you'll need a behind the music style documentary to catch up with all their shit." Marcus said between bites of his food.

"OMG, what happened now Bryce?" she asked.

"Oh you mean before or after he fucked Erica West and Mia caught them cuddled up at the back to school event?" Marcus blurted out.

"Bryce!" she said with a look of shock on her face.

"Yeah it's a lil' crazy between us right now, I'll catch you up on all that later. But what's up with my birthday party? What you got planned?"

"Yeah I was telling her that you should do it in the Georgia Dome this year," an overzealous Marcus said.

"He ain't graduating from high school dummy, it's his birthday," she said.

"So what you got for me Eva?" Bryce asked.

"Ok I was thinking we could do a masquerade ball style event at the Georgia Aquarium What do you think?" Eva asked looking at Bryce, the smile on his face giving away his answer.

"Yeah, that sounds nice." He replied while rubbing his hands together. Eva had peaked his interest and he couldn't wait to see how she pulled this one off.

"Aquarium..." Marcus chimed in, "yeah that's fly. Ah, you think you get some fine ass mermaid bitches to swim around in those tanks?" causing both Bryce and Eva to just shake their heads.

* * *

"Your honor, in light of this new evidence, I motion for an immediate dismissal of all charges against my client," Mia said as the courtroom erupted.

"Order in the court, order in this court!" the judge shouted, as he banged his gavel to silence the noise in his courtroom. "Motion granted, all charges against the defendant are dismissed and he is to be released from custody effective immediately."

Mia turned and made eye contact with the defendant's elderly grandmother who was sitting in the front row of the courtroom with tears running down her face. When the lady saw she had Mia's attention she mouthed the words "Thank you." Mia just nodded her head and smiled before walking over to her desk to gather her papers. When she got to the desk she reached her hand out to shake the young defendant's hand and he grabbed her and almost hugged the air out her lungs.

Mia was standing out in the lobby of the courtroom talking with the young man and his grandmother when she noticed a familiar face walk out of the courtroom amongst a group of people walking towards her. She finished up with the young man and his grandmother then walked over to where the man was standing waiting to talk with her.

"So what are you doing here Mr. Bradshaw?" she asked him.

"Just wanted to come see you do your thing and see if all they say about the great Mia Armstrong was true."

"And?"

"I was very impressed. You really are the pit bull in a skirt they say you are."

"Oh is that what they are calling me now? A bitch?" she said as she shot him an evil look.

"No, I didn't mean it like that, I was just saying..." he said as he scrambled trying to find the words to explain his previous statement.

"No I'm just kidding. Look at you sweating and

stuttering. I hope that's not how you behave in court. I would hate to be your client," she teased.

"You enjoy giving me a hard time huh?"

"That's because you make it so easy, Mr. Bradshaw."

"Christion," he replied. "Call me Christion."

"Oh I know your name, I just was waiting on you to give me permission to use it," she continued to tease.

"Oh you really a comedian," he said.

"What can I say I'm multi-talented, but anyway did Angela send that list to you?"

"Yeah, I got it. Thanks again."

"No problem."

"So what are you gonna do to celebrate? Anything special planned?" he inquired.

"No not really, I'm just gonna meet up with a couple of my girlfriends at FAB and have a couple drinks. You're more than welcome to come if you like."

"That sounds good, but I don't want to intrude on you and your girls," he said.

"You wouldn't be intruding at all," she said.

"You sure?"

"Yes, now come on before I change my mind," she joked.

* * *

Kim and Latrice were sitting at a table enjoying a laugh when they spotted Mia and an unknown male companion enter the restaurant. Both women couldn't help but notice how good looking the man was. His goatee and beard was neatly trimmed and complimented his unblemished brown skin. He sported a low taper and stood just over 6 feet tall with a muscular frame. He was dressed in a long sleeve white button up with a pair of tan dress pants and a pair of cognac colored dress shoes. The two women stopped laughing as Mia and her guest reached the table.

"I see you heifers started without me," Mia said, as she noticed the half empty glasses of wine and open bottle sitting on the table.

"Yeah and we see you brought a guest," Latrice said, as she eyed him and gave him the once over.

"Yes, Latrice and Kim this is Christion Bradshaw. He's a new lawyer at the firm. Christion these are my best friends, Latrice and Kim."

"Hello ladies, it's nice to meet ya'll," he said as he reached out and shook each of their hands before sitting down.

"So what were ya'll laughing at?" Mia asked as she sat down.

"Oh, Latrice was telling me about something that happened at the shop today," Kim said.

"What happened? I wanna know." Mia asked.

"I'll tell you later. Right now I wanna know some more about you Mr. Christion Bradshaw," Latrice said.

"What is it that you would like to know?" he asked.

"Do you have a woman?" Latrice boldly asked.

"Latrice!" Kim said. "Please forgive my friend, she left her meds at home."

"It's ok, but to answer your question, no I don't," he said.

"So where are you from and what made you move here?" Kim asked.

"How you know I'm not from here?" he asked.

"Your accent is a dead giveaway," she responded.

"Ha-ha ok, well I'm from Harlem."

"Oh ok, so how you like Atlanta so far?" Latrice asked.

"So far, so good. Aside from your friend over here giving me a hard time at work, everything has been good," he said.

"I just give him a hard time about not knowing his way around the city that's all," Mia said.

"Well you have to forgive her; she hasn't been getting any lately," Latrice said causing Mia to almost choke on her drink.

"Ok you've had enough," Kim said as she reached to take Latrice's glass from her causing it to spill over and get on Christion's shirt.

"Oh my god, I am so sorry," Kim said.

"Oh me too." Latrice said.

"It's ok, where's the restroom at?" he said.

"That way," Mia said and pointed him in the right direction.

As he disappeared the two friends started with their

interrogation of Mia.

"Girl, what is going on with that? He is fine as hell. So when did you start fucking him?" Latrice asked.

"It's not even like that Latrice. He is new to the city and he is pretty cool so I was just trying to show him around a lil' bit," Mia responded.

"Show him around or show him off? Shit if you don't want him, make sure you show him where I live 'cause you acting like you don't know what to do with his fine ass," Latrice said.

"I'm not blind Trice. He is a very good looking man. But that doesn't mean I have to sleep with him," Mia explained to her.

"That's right plus you don't need to be getting involved right now. You just got out of a relationship," Kim said.

"Who said anything about a relationship? I'm talking about having some fun. I know you still not waiting around on Bryce to get his shit together?" Latrice asked.

"It has nothing to do with Bryce," Mia said.

"It always has something to do with Bryce," Latrice said.

"Hey ya'll here he comes," Kim said as she looked up and saw Christion returning.

"So was I gone long enough for ya'll to finish talking about me?" he asked upon his return, causing the women to laugh. "So are you ladies ready to order? My treat."

"Oh I like you already," Latrice said.

"Yeah let's order because I have to be home to get the kids off the bus soon," Kim said.

As Mia sat there eating her food she couldn't help but think about what her friends had said about Christion. After all he was fine and he was single. Maybe she did need to just have a little fun, nothing serious. But there was still something deep down inside of her that wanted to give Bryce another chance or at least hear him out. She knew that until she fully addressed their situation those feelings would never go away.

CHAPTER FOUR

Bryce had just begun to work up a sweat on the treadmill when his phone rang at 6 a.m. he knew it could only be one person. When he looked at his phone his thoughts were confirmed; it was Yolanda, the only person who beat him to work every day. He grabbed the remote and turned the music down in his state of the art home gym, then put his bluetooth in his ear and answered.

"Good morning Yolanda."

"Good morning Mr. Edwards, I'm sorry for bothering you so early. It's just I didn't know if you were coming into the office today because you hadn't returned my email. I got a call from Ms. Cozier's assistant this morning saying that Ms. Cozier had an unexpected issue come up and that she would have to cancel the meeting for next week."

"Oh really?" Bryce said with a hint of disappointment in his voice.

"Yes, but she wanted to know if there would be any way to maybe move the meeting up. She said she would be free on Saturday, if it's not an inconvenience."

"Saturday? As in 2 days from now?" he asked.

"Yes and she wants you to fly to her. Her assistant said this might be the only time to meet this month," she explained.

"Ok, tell her that's not a problem. Saturday will be fine.

"Got it, anything else?" she asked.

"Oh yeah, could you call the florist and have them send some roses over to Mia's office. Tell them to put "congratulations on the big win" on the card. Send a dozen in each color."

"Ok."

"Thanks Yolanda, you're the best."

"I know," she joked before hanging up.

Bryce laughed as he hung up and continued his early morning workout. It had been almost two weeks since he was last in his home gym and about the same amount of time since he had actually been home. Home was a 14,000 square foot ultra-luxury estate named Edwards Manor that Bryce had built 8 months ago. The 8 bedroom, 9 bathroom estate had a massive chef style kitchen, bowling alley, indoor basketball gym, an infinity pool with a hot tub and a home theater— where Bryce spent most of his time in the house. He rarely slept in his massive master bedroom, most nights he fell asleep in his favorite recliner up front watching ESPN. The house staff always knew where to look if they couldn't find him. Bryce employed close to 15 people at Edwards Manor which included a chef, housekeepers, ground workers and security. Bryce had the basement of the house turned into his own personal showroom floor for his many vehicles and it resembled the bat cave from the Batman movies. He even had the entrance built into a large rock that opened up at the touch of a button to let him in then closed up and looked as if nothing was there. There was also a guest house on the property that Bryce allowed some of his famous friends to use when they were in town and wanted to remain low key.

Bryce walked down the hallway into the kitchen were his chef had prepared his favorite breakfast— a cheese steak omelet and home fried potatoes. This was one of the things he missed when he stayed at the penthouse downtown, Chef Annie's great cooking. She cooked regardless if he was there or not, she made sure all the employees ate every day. Bryce had been eating meals prepared by her for as long as he could remember. She knew all his favorite foods, desserts and snacks and she kept his refrigerator full of them all. As he sat on one of the expensive marble stools built in front of the breakfast bar eating, Chef Annie finished chopping up some fresh fruit and put some in a bowl then placed it on the bar in front of him. Bryce finished up his breakfast and his talk with Chef Annie before heading upstairs to take a shower and get dressed.

* * *

Bryce pulled into his parking spot at the job and made his way up to his office. He said good morning to everyone he passed in the hallway only stopping to chat with Yolanda briefly before entering his office. Now that Natasha Cozier's meeting had been moved up to Saturday, he had a lot of work to do and only a short time to do it in. He really wanted her to work on this project with him and he knew she was high in demand so to actually get a meeting with her was an accomplishment, but he also knew he had one shot and one shot only at peaking her interest in the project. He called Marcus who was on his way in and told him that once he got in to come straight to his office to help him. The two worked non-stop on the proposal for hours. They were nearing completion when Yolanda interrupted them to tell Bryce he had a phone call.

"Mr. Edwards you have a call on line 1."

"Ah, can take a message and tell who ever it is that I'll call them back."

"I think you might want to take this one, it's Mia."

Bryce paused and looked over at Marcus who seemed just as surprised as him. He walked over to his desk and sat down before saying, "Ok, thanks Yolanda I got it." He pressed the blinking light on his phone. "Hello."

"Hello Bryce," Mia responded.

"Mia," Bryce said as if he hadn't known it was her.

"Please Bryce, I know Yolanda told you who it was on the phone. So don't try to act like you didn't know it was me."

"Ok, you got me. So what's going on Mia? You keeping things real formal by calling my office aren't you?"

"I was just calling to say thanks for the roses. I figured it was the least I could do," she stated coldly.

"Wow, anyway I've been calling your office like you asked, but I seem not to be able to ever get you on the phone."

"Well if you've been watching the news and I know you have," she said sarcastically referring to his relationship with Erica West, "you can see that I've been pretty busy."

"Yeah I have, that's how I know that you're not so busy now. So how about that meeting?"

"What about it?" she asked.

"Damn Mia, stop giving me the run around. Either you want to meet and talk about things or you don't. Which is it?" he said beginning to become frustrated with her games.

"Ok, Bryce its 12:50 right now, I don't have my next

appointment until 3:00. I'm free until then, so if you can manage to pick up some food and bring it with you we can have lunch and talk."

"Can do, so what would you like to eat?"

"Justin's, already called and ordered they are expecting you," she said before hanging up.

Angela led Bryce into Mia's empty office and directed him to a lounge area with a couple chairs, small couch and coffee table. She told him that Mia would be with him shortly before exiting the room. He looked around the room. Mia had changed it a lot since the last time he had been there. He immediately thought to himself that she must have changed it when she changed her look. Just like her new hairstyle he liked the new look of the office. As he was admiring the painting on the wall behind her desk, the office door opened and Mia walked in. Bryce once again couldn't help but notice how good she looked with her new haircut and how sexy she was standing there in a white blouse and tan skirt that hugged all her curves. Mia was a beautiful Georgia peach. She stood about 5'8 with light brown skin and light brown almond shaped eyes. Although she never played a sport a day in her life, she had the body of a female track star with the ass to match. Her beautiful smile could melt the coldest heart but being on her bad side was the one place in the world you didn't want to be. She was an intelligent, strong minded, fearless and extremely stubborn woman who loved hard and hated harder. Bryce knew the last two all too well.

"Hello Mia, it's nice to see you again," he said as she closed the door behind her. "You're looking beautiful like always."

"Thanks," she answered. "So did you make sure they put napkins in the bag?" she said as she walked towards the bags on the coffee table purposely changing the subject.

"Yes I did and I got you an orange soda, not a lot of ice," he said nicely trying to ignore her coldness.

Mia smiled on the inside because that was how she liked it and she hadn't even asked for it, but she still kept on her poker face. "So are you gonna stand up the whole time or are you gonna sit down and eat?"

Bryce made his way over to the couch and sat next to her as she removed the food from the bags along with the forks and napkins. She handed him his food then began to enjoy hers.

"So what have you been up to these past few months?" he asked.

"Nothing much just the trial, that case really consumed most of my time," she answered between bites.

"Speaking of, you did a great job getting that kid acquitted. I don't know how much it means to you at this moment, but I want you to know that I'm so proud of you. I know how serious you take your job and how hard you work at your craft and it's good to see what is happening with your career."

"Thank you Bryce. Believe it or not that really means a lot to hear you say that," she said.

"So aside from the trial what else have you been up to?" Bryce asked trying to find out if she had been seeing somebody.

"Nothing, why Bryce? Why don't you ask what you really want to know?"

"And what is it that you think I wanna know?"

"You wanna know if I been dating somebody or somebodies."

"Well have you?"

"Why, and if I have?"

"Well if you have..."

"Well if I have it's none of your business. What are you worried for anyway you don't want me."

"See here you go."

"Here I go what? That's the truth ain't it? You've moved on already so why do you even care what I'm doing?"

"Moved on? What are you talking about Mia?"

"Erica West, you're fucking her aren't you? I know you are so don't even lie."

"Mia I didn't come here to argue with you or lie to you."

"So what did you come here for huh? You didn't come to propose. You wanted to be single so I gave you what you wanted. Why are you here? What am I missing?" she asked as she felt her heart starting to beat fast as she tried to hold back her tears. She began thinking to herself how this was a bad idea. Maybe she shouldn't have agreed to meet with him; maybe it was still too soon for her.

"Mia what you're missing is that I didn't want to marry you, but I didn't want to be single," Bryce said.

"What are you talking about?" a confused Mia asked.

"Mia I love you with all my heart so I was just being honest with you. I really didn't know you would take it as if I didn't want to be with you. I just feel like marriage is a serious step and nobody should take that step unless they are 100% ready. Anything less than that leaves to much opportunity for something bad to happen. I only see myself marrying you but I want to be able to give you 100% of me when I do," he explained.

"But I feel you have been," she said.

"But I know I haven't been and that's the important thing."

"What do you mean? What is it that's holding you back from giving me all of you? Is it another woman, what is it? Are you hiding something from me, do you have a baby you haven't told me about?" she asked as tears began rolling down her cheek.

"No it's nothing like that I promise," he assured her.

"So what is it Bryce?" she asked.

Just then her office phone began to ring breaking them out of the deep conversation they were locked in. Bryce grabbed her hand attempting to stop her from answering it, but then he let it go realizing that they were in her place of business and it could be important. As she tended to her phone call Bryce thought back to the ride home after the night at the comedy club. He remembered saying to himself that there were so many things he wanted to tell her and that if she gave him the chance he would. He now found himself with that very chance, but somehow he still couldn't bring himself to tell her all the things he needed to. It wasn't that he didn't want to, it was just that he didn't know how she would take it and he wasn't ready to risk it. As he stared at her talking on the phone his mind began thinking back to all the times they had wild passionate sex almost any and everywhere and he began to get aroused. Mia's round juicy ass poking out of her tight skirt wasn't helping either. Mia hung up the phone and immediately picked it up and called Angela's desk and told her to hold the rest of her calls until her meeting was over. She hadn't even noticed that Bryce was now standing directly behind her. As she hung up the phone, he put his arms around her waist and pulled her to him and started kissing her on the back of her neck. His warm wet lips against her neck felt so good, she tried to resist him but it was already too late. He went right to the spot on her neck that he knew drove her crazy and she could already feel herself getting moist. The more he licked and kissed her the more she realized how much she missed him touching her body; just the thought made her grind her fat ass against his now rock hard dick. She reached her hand around and started rubbing it through his pants. Bryce turned her around so that they were now face to face and he started to unbutton her blouse revealing her black Victoria Secret bra and her beautiful breasts. He began kissing on the top of her breasts as she raised her dress up around her waist. He then removed her panties, lifted her up and sat her on top of her desk, then dove face first into her now dripping wet pussy. Mia couldn't help but let out a moan as his tongue stroked every inch of her pussy and he sucked on her clit until she reached an orgasmic state. Bryce unbuttoned his pants and let them fall around his ankles, pulled his swollen dick from his boxers and slowly buried it deep inside of Mia's warm, wet juice box causing her to grip the sides of her desk as she laid back and enjoyed every stroke. Bryce was so turned on; not only by how good the sex was but by the fact that someone could walk into her office and catch them at any time. He began to stroke faster and harder causing Mia to moan more as she began cumming. Bryce's body began to tighten up as he felt himself nearing his climax. Just then Mia sat up on the desk and pushed him off of her.

"Yo what's wrong? What happened? Why you do that?"

he asked confused by what had just occurred.

"How long are we gonna do this Bryce?" she asked.

"You said your next appointment isn't til 3 right? So at least til then," he said.

"No I don't mean this, I mean this. The back and forth, break up to make up shit. Where is this going? What are we doing? Are we starting something just to have it end bad again?" she asked back to back sounding like the lawyer she was.

"Huh?" Bryce said still confused at what was happening.

"Exactly! You can't answer the important questions."

"What! Hold up Mia you're buggin'. First of all stop with the lawyer routine. I thought we both were just enjoying what was happening," he said as he pulled up his pants.

"Is that why you came here Bryce just to try and have sex with me?" she said as she got down off of her desk and began fixing her clothes.

"For one I don't think I was trying to have sex with you, I was. And two, no that wasn't my plan coming here. I came here to try and give you some type of understanding of what happened between us and to hopefully work things out, but I see now this wasn't a good idea."

"No it wasn't and I think you should leave now," she said as she sat down behind her desk.

"I was just thinking the same thing," he said.

CHAPTER FIVE

Mia pulled into an open parking spot in front of Beauty Mark, the hair and makeup salon owned by Latrice. Every Saturday morning the three best friends would get their hair done, sip wine, and gossip. She walked through the door and was greeted by the sound of Maxwell's "Pretty Wings" playing on the salon's sound system; the girl at the front desk greeted her and began walking her to the back. Latrice had opened her shop almost 3 years ago and it had grown into one of the most popular salons in the city. It was very upscale and the look was inspired by some of the salons she had visited on South Beach all the way down to the 16 inch plasma screens at every station. They also had some of the best stylist in the city. The best being Twan, the over the top homosexual, who was also the Wendy Williams of the shop. Mia sat in his chair next to Kim and Latrice who were already being worked on.

"Late as usual Ms. Thang," he said when she sat down.

"No darling, I had to make an entrance," she said with a smile.

"I know that's right, honey!" he said as they slapped five.

"Whatever bitch," Latrice said interrupting their moment. "Did you bring the wine?"

"Yes, don't I always," Mia replied.

"Shanice bring us some glasses please," Latrice said to one of the other stylist.

"Kim where's my beautiful niece at? Why didn't you bring her? You know that's my baby," Mia asked

"Her daddy took her and her brother to their grandmother's house," Kim replied.

"So Mia what's been going on? I saw you on TV all week looking fabulous," Twan said.

"Same old, same old. Just trying to keep the innocent ones free."

"Gurl, I wish somebody would come and lock me up. I know I could finds me a man in there boo-boo," Twan stated causing them all to laugh. "My home girl told me her man came home from doing 6 years in jail and he wanted her to do all type of stuff to his butt that they wasn't doing before. Hmm honey, put me in a cell with who was doing that to him cuz I would be a willing participant."

"Ok, ok that's enough Twan. Don't nobody wanna hear that mess," Latrice proclaimed.

"Whatever hater," he snapped back. "You just mad cuz I look better than you."

"Please."

"You are too much Twan," Mia said.

"So Mia you said you would tell us about your meeting with Bryce when we got here so spill it," Kim said.

"Yeah spill it." Latrice added.

"Well I agreed to meet with him at my office on Thursday."

"Why so you wouldn't fuck him?" Latrice blurted out.

"Anyway he came up and we started talking. He was trying to justify his reason for doing what he did."

"So what did he say?" Kim asked.

"He said what you said he would say; that he was just being honest with me when he said he wasn't ready to get married and that him not wanting to get married didn't mean he didn't want to marry me it just meant he wasn't ready. He said him getting married to me and not being ready would actually cause more problems than it would solve."

"See I told you," Kim said with a smile.

"Yeah you were right."

"Hold on, you mean to tell me you fell for that shit?"

Latrice said.

"I didn't say I fell for anything, I'm just explaining what happened."

"Mia, did you sleep with him?" Latrice asked.

"Huh?" Mia said caught off guard by the question.

"Oh damn Mia, you did didn't you?" Latrice said as she banged her hand on the arm of the chair.

"Yeah but..."

"But what Mia?'

"It wasn't like that, it just happened. But I stopped it before it went too far. Then I told him he had to leave. I actually was a little too hard on him."

"Sound like he was the one hard," Twan said.

"Why Mia? Why'd you sleep wit' him? What was all the breaking up for then, Bryce needs to learn a lesson. He can kick that bullshit about only wanting to marry you, but Bryce wants to have his cake and eat it too. He wants you to play the wife role and take care of him when he is sick and all that other stuff but he still wants to live like a bachelor."

"Calm down Trice. Bryce really loves Mia and it's obvious she still have those types of feelings for him. Those feelings just don't go away by staying away from him for a couple of months. Those feelings have to run their course, good or bad," Kim intervened.

"What you know about these men nowadays Kim? You been out the game for how long now?" Latrice asked.

"I don't know about the game, but I know about the ups and downs of love. That's why I've been married to the same man for the last nine years. And you've had how many men in that time? Exactly," Kim said as she put Latrice in her place. "Mia what is it that you want, why did you kick him out?"

"I don't know I just had so many things running through my head at the time. I just needed him to go so I could sort them out," she said.

"Well have you?" Kim asked.

"Girl I'm even more confused now," Mia said laughing. "My heart is telling me to give him another chance, but my mind says something different."

"Well go with your heart but don't be a fool," Kim said.

"Yeah don't be a dumb ass," Latrice said. "But go with your heart girl and we got your back no matter what happens."

* * *

The black SUV that picked Bryce up when his private jet landed pulled up in front of Mr. Chow's. Bryce had been up most of the night finalizing the details and working on his pitch, but after catching some sleep on the flight he was well rested. He took a deep breath before opening the door and stepping out. Upon entering the restaurant he was immediately led to a table that had been reserved for him. As Bryce sat alone waiting for his guest to show up, he took the leisure of ordering himself a drink while he waited. He loved New York; he enjoyed himself every time he had the chance to come to the city of bright lights and big stars. He hadn't been in a while and for a moment he thought about staying to enjoy some of the nightlife it had to offer, but eventually decided against it. He hadn't even noticed the fact that it was now almost 8:30 p.m and Natasha Cozier hadn't shown yet. Once he looked at his watch and saw the time he chalked it up to New York City traffic. Another 15 minutes passed before he started to think that maybe she wouldn't show. His nervousness disappeared once he looked up and saw the beautiful woman who looked like she had been snatched off a runway heading towards his table.   Nervous energy was instantly replaced with disbelief and amazement as he stared at her. He had seen pictures of her in magazines and he had seen her on TV, but none of that compared to seeing her beauty in person. The Dominican and Jamaican blood running through her veins had really created something appealing to look at. Her light brown skin was flawless and her jet black hair flowed down her back—with lips like Angelina Jolie and light brown eyes that could hypnotize any man who stared into them too long. She was slim built but very curvy and by far one of the hottest women Bryce had laid his eyes on. He stood to greet her as she arrived at the table. The waiter noticed Bryce's guest had arrived and came over to ask if they were ready to order. They both ordered without having to look at the menu. They made small talk until their food arrived then Bryce began his pitch. For the next twenty five minutes he thoroughly went over all the details of the project with her, from ideas to timetables and most importantly the cost.

After all was said and done she reached her hand across the table and said, "I'm onboard. Send the contracts over to my lawyers and when that's finalized we can began."

"That's exactly what I hoped you'd say," Bryce said as he shook her hand and flashed his multimillion dollar smile. "Now let's celebrate, how about a bottle of champagne?"

"Not really the champagne type. How 'bout a bottle of Patrón?"

"Patrón it is."

As the two sat celebrating the making of a deal over shots, the conversation began to take a more personal turn.

"So Bryce I've noticed that you're not wearing a ring, so there's not a Mrs. Edwards waiting for you back at home?" she asked.

"Nah, no Mrs. Edwards at home."

"So is there a Ms. Anybody waiting at home for you?" she asked.

"Are you asking if I'm single?"

"Yeah, are you?"

"Unfortunately, yes I am."

"Unfortunately," she repeated with a laugh.

"Why, what's so funny?" he asked.

"Because I'm sure that Bryce Edwards doesn't have a problem finding a woman."

"What makes you so sure of that?"

"I've heard stories."

"Stories?"

"Yeah I've done my research. And from what I've heard, you have nothing to be ashamed of."

Bryce was caught off guard by her last statement but he was not about to let her get the upper hand in this mental game of chess. "Yeah that's funny you say that because I've done some research myself and from what I've heard you don't have a problem finding a woman either," he said with a slight grin on his face as if to say checkmate.

She smiled before answering. "What can I say, I love sex. I'm sure a man like you can appreciate that."

"I can."

"And when I see something I want I go after it, man or woman. Like now," she said as she stared at him like her prey.

Bryce now found himself in an awkward position. Any other time he would have jumped at the chance at a night of wild freaky sex with a woman as beautiful as Natasha Cozier. But no matter how tempted he was, especially after what had happened with Mia, he knew mixing business with pleasure was a definite mistake. His only problem was how would he say no to her advances without blowing the deal.

"So Bryce how about we take care of the bill and we continue our research a little more in depth back at my penthouse."

"As much as I would love to get deep into some research with you, I really have to be getting back to Atlanta. I made a promise to my aunt that I really must keep, so I have to get back and get some sleep because I'm sure if I stay neither one of us will."

"A man who keeps his promises, I see I'm gonna like working with you already," she said assuring him that despite her failed attempt at seducing him she still intended on working with him in the future as well as continuing her pursuit.

"And please allow me to take care of the bill, it's the least I can do," he said as he reached for his wallet.

* * *

"Yeah I just landed. The meeting went great. I'll fill you in on the details once I reach the crib. Trust me you're going to want to hear this." Bryce hung up with Marcus just as his private jet came to a stop. What had been a clear afternoon sky upon his take-off was now a nasty stormy Atlanta night. When the plane door opened Bryce descended the steps and was met at the bottom by the driver of the SUV that Yolanda had scheduled to pick him up. The driver was holding an open umbrella to escort him to the waiting vehicle. Bryce really didn't like being driven around especially in his own town. He preferred to do the driving but on a night like this, after two flights and a meeting, he enjoyed being able to relax. The ride home was a quiet one, with Bryce and his driver barely saying two words to each other. He spent most of his time on his phone checking sports' scores and emails. As he scrolled down he recognized a certain email address that he hadn't seen in a while, it was Mia's personal email but before he could open it and read it the silence in the car was broken by the driver.

"Mr. Edwards, I don't mean to bother you sir but I think the car behind us has been following us ever since we left the airport."

"Are you sure?" Bryce asked as he looked out the back window trying to get a look at the car and the driver. But with the heavy rain all he could see were headlights.

"I'm almost certain."

"Ok, well let's make sure. Get off at the next exit."

The driver did as Bryce said and got off at the next exit. So did the headlights that the driver thought was following him.

"Ok now make a left and go two lights up and make a right," Bryce told the driver as he looked out the back window seeing if the headlights would follow and they did. Now he was sure he was being followed. Bryce continued to give directions to the driver; he was taking him the back way to his house. Just then the headlights sped up and rammed the back of the SUV and Bryce screamed at the driver to drive faster. The headlights remained right on their tail ramming the truck again and again. Bryce tried his best to remain calm so the driver would too, but by the look on the man's face it wasn't working. He told him that they would have to make a left two streets up. As they made the turn the headlights rammed into them again causing the SUV to slide into the turn. Bryce knew at the speed they were driving, mixed with the wet roads, the chances of this ending good were slim to none. He grabbed the seatbelt, which he didn't like to wear, and strapped himself in just as another turn was approaching. Before they could get into the turn, the headlights rammed them again, this time causing the driver to lose control as the truck began spinning.As the truck slid off the road and down a hill, it began to flip several times before coming to a stop upside down. Bryce heard the tires of the car that had been chasing them screeching off in the distance just before everything went black.

CHAPTER SIX

The car had barely come to a stop when the two boys jumped out and ran towards the front door of the massive beach front home. Bryce couldn't wait to show Tremaine all the cool things the house had to offer. Mr. Edwards yelled for the boys to come help with the bags but they had already disappeared into the house. Tremaine followed Bryce all through the house not saying a word, he was still trying to soak it all in. He stared out of one of the giant windows, in what was to be his room during the stay, at the clear blue water and sand on the beach behind the house. He had never seen a beach before or had his own room. He had never been out of the city limits of Atlanta and now he was on the beaches of St. Thomas and he couldn't believe his eyes.

"Yo Tre come on let me show you the rest of the house," Bryce yelled as he stood in the doorway of the room breaking his friends daydream. "Oh yeah bring your swimming trunks."

"Oh man, they in my bag which is still in the car," Tre said.

"Don't worry about it. The bags will be up in a minute. You wanna go ride dirt bikes instead? We could go swimming later."

"Ok. But can we grab a sandwich first? I'm a lil' hungry."

"Yeah come on."

The two boys ran downstairs to the kitchen where Trina, the residence's housekeeper, was stocking the refrigerator with groceries. She told them she would fix them anything they wanted once she finished. While they sat and waited they were joined in the kitchen by Mr. Edwards.

"Hey dad," Bryce said as his father entered the kitchen.

"Hey Mr. Edwards," Tre said.

"Hey fellas, I didn't think I would see you two for a while the way you guys ran off," Mr. Edwards said. "But I should have known I'd find you in here bothering Trina already."

"It's ok, they are growing boys and they got to eat ya know," Trina said in her thick island accent. "Now you don't get too full off these sandwiches Bryce. I'm making your favorite; oxtails, peas and rice tonight."

"I can't wait," Bryce said as his face lit up with a smile. "You ever ate that before Tre?"

"Nah."

"Dad where's mom?" Bryce asked.

"Oh your mother is laying down resting. You know how she is after traveling." Mr. Edwards replied.

"Oh, well me and Tre are gonna go ride the dirt bikes on the *beach for a lil' while. We'll be back."* Bryce said as the two boys ran *out of the kitchen.*

"Ok, you boys be careful and make sure you wear those helmets," Mr. Edwards yelled to them. *"Bryce do you hear me? Bryce. Bryce...*

* * *

"Bryce, Bryce, Bryce can you hear me?"

Bryce slowly opened his eyes as he realized that he wasn't dreaming anymore. Somebody was really calling his name. The sound of his name being called seemed to enter his ear and bounce around in his head and echo louder and louder causing the headache he already had to get worse. As he opened his eyes the lights from the room didn't help either. His vision was blurry and he couldn't quite make out the face of the person that had been calling his name, but as he stared at them more his eyes slowly started to focus and he could see it was Marcus.

"Aw man it's good to see you woke up. How you feel?" Marcus asked.

"Like shit," Bryce said stating the obvious. "Where am I and what happened?"

"You're in the hospital, you were in a bad car accident. Your truck slid off the road and flipped a couple of times. You're lucky to be alive, you don't remember?"

"Vaguely, is anybody else hurt, what about the driver?"

Bryce asked.

"He didn't make it. He was thrown from the car and died at the scene." Marcus sadly informed Bryce.

"Aw shit, does anybody know if he has family? Has someone contacted them?" Bryce asked.

"I don't know man. I been getting information as it's been given to me. I called Mia and left a message on her phone."

"Man I'm in so much pain."

"The nurse that was in here said you got a concussion, a couple of broken ribs and your left leg is broke."

"That would explain why I feel like I was tackled by Ray Lewis."

"So you don't remember anything about the crash?" Marcus asked.

"I remember talking to you on the phone. I remember getting in the truck and checking my emails. I remember seeing really bright headlights, then I remember just waking up here."

"Damn that's it?"

"Yeah. Turn on the news see what they are saying maybe that will help."

Marcus walked over and turned on the TV as Bryce managed to push the button on the bed lifting him up so he could get a better view.

"Good evening, this is James Summers for channel 12 news

and I'm reporting live from the scene of tonight's deadly accident involving multi-millionaire real estate developer, Bryce Edwards. Police originally believed that the bad weather may have been the cause of the accident but now they are saying that the SUV that was carrying Mr. Edwards may have been run off the road by another vehicle that fled the scene. More details as they come in, reporting live for channel 12 news I'm James Summers."

"Watching the competition I see," said the voice coming from the woman standing in the door.

"Erica. What are you doing here? Shouldn't you be out there trying to get the scoop? Or is that why you're here?" Bryce asked with a look of suspicion on his face.

"No that's not why I'm here, this is a personal visit. I came as soon as I heard." she said as she stepped inside of the room and made her way over to his bed side.

"Thanks that means a lot." Bryce said.

"Why are you thanking me silly, isn't that what friends do?"

"I guess it is. Speaking of friends, Erica this is my best friend Marcus Gilyard, Marcus this is Erica West."

"Hey how are you doing? I saw you on TV a few times you do good work." Marcus said as he stuck his hand out to shake hers.

"Thank you, it's nice to meet you."

"So they are saying somebody ran you off the road, why

would somebody do that to you? Makes no sense." Marcus said shifting his focus back to the news report.

"I don't know maybe it was a random thing, you know like a drunk driver or something." Bryce said.

"Oh my goodness, look at you, you are all bruised and scraped up. And your leg, you look like you are in so much pain."

"I know, but the good news is I feel worse than I look." Bryce said trying to make a joke.

"It's gonna be ok, if I have to come up here every day and nurse you back to health myself you know I will," she said as she leaned over and kissed him on the forehead.

"Oh yeah?" a voice said causing everyone in the room to turn towards the door.

"Mia," Bryce said as he saw her standing there looking like she had been crying the whole ride there.

"I can't believe it. Here I am crying my eyes out and praying to God that you are ok so I can get up here and tell you how sorry I am for being so hard on you lately. But now that I see you're ok and you're being taken care of," she said as she stared at Erica. "There's really no need for me to be here."

"Mia," Bryce said.

"Maybe I should go." Erica said.

"No you stay. It's obvious I'm the one out of place. Have a nice life Bryce." Mia said as she turned and exited the room.

"Mia no don't leave." Bryce yelled sending an agonizing pain through his ribs causing him to lay back on the bed in pain.

"Ok, everybody has to go," the nurse said as she rushed in the room. "He needs his rest and he can't be getting all excited."

"Ok I'm gonna get out of here," Erica said. "You get some rest and I will call you."

"Yeah I'm gone too man, I'll be back to see you tomorrow." Marcus said.

Bryce just nodded his head as the pain medicine the nurse injected him with began to kick in.

* * *

Mia's heart was still pounding in her chest as she stepped off the elevator into the hospital's lobby. Still wiping tears away, she opened her handbag and began frantically searching for her keys. Never bothering to look up she hadn't noticed the familiar face she had just passed as she made her way through the doors and to the parking lot.

"Mia, Hey Mia! Mia hold up."

She almost reached her car before she realized that someone had been calling her name. As she turned to see who it was, she quickly recognized the man jogging towards her.

"Christion," she said as she tried to compose herself not wanting him to see her in such an emotional state.

"Hey Mia, what's going on? You just zoomed pass me in the lobby. Is everything alright?"

"Yeah everything is ok." she said as she wiped her face for any remaining tears.

"You sure? Cuz you don't look like it. I'm saying, if you need to talk or anything like that, I know you don't know me that well but I'm a pretty good listener."

"Well I'll keep that in mind, but no seriously I'm ok."

"You sure?" he asked again clearly indicating he didn't believe a word she was saying.

"Yes I am, really," she said trying to sound as believable as possible. "But thanks for your concern," she continued as she opened her door and got into her car.

"No problem, I guess I'll see you on Monday then."

"Bright and early."

"Yeah don't remind me," he said causing her to crack a slight smile.

"Ok you have a goodnight."

"You too," he replied as he watched her pull out of her parking space and continue out of the parking lot.

Mia drove onto the parking ramp of her building, pulled into her parking space and cut her engine off. She had made it home in what felt like no time, with so much on her mind it almost felt like the car had drove itself home. She had just recently purchased one of the luxurious condos in the midtown high rise after deciding to rent her 3-level town home out. She hadn't even had the chance to have a house warming yet. That thought hadn't crossed her mind as she entered her home, removed her coat and headed straight for the kitchen and the bottle of Moscato in her wine chiller. She grabbed a wine glass from the cabinet and headed towards her bedroom. She walked through her room into the bathroom and sat the bottle of wine and glass on the edge of the tub before turning on the water. She poured a few drops of her Victoria Secrets "Forever Blushing" bath gel into her sunken tub and entered the walk-in closet on the opposite side of the bathroom as it continued to fill the tub and air with the sweet but calm aroma. Mia reemerged from the closet wearing nothing but a towel. She cut off the water, dropped the towel and stepped in the tub. She grabbed the bottle of wine and poured some in her glass. She hit the button turning on the jets in the tub, took a sip of wine, laid back and began crying as the thought of her on again off again relationship with Bryce finally coming to an end began sinking in. She knew it was time to turn the page on this chapter in her life but it was easier said than done. She had been in love with this man for the better part of a decade, almost since the first day they met in high school. She had shared all her hopes, dreams, fears and insecurities with him through the years and wanted nothing more than to be his wife and mother of his children. But she was convinced now more than ever that that was a dream they did not share. Bryce was too caught up in the high flying, the fast cars and the flocks of beautiful women throwing themselves at him to be anybody's husband. He loved the title of being one of the world's most eligible bachelors more than he loved her. She deserved better and refused to play second fiddle to his fame and lifestyle. The day had sent her through a gauntlet of emotions. First thinking she had been too hard on him, then thinking she had lost him, only to get the hospital and see him in the arms of another woman. "Fuck Bryce, that bitch can have him. Let her nurse his ass back to health." She thought to herself just as she began to feel short of breath and her heart started to pound in her chest. Mia recognized the feeling immediately, so she stepped out of the tub and began drying off as fast as possible. She could feel her mind start to race and her body temperature seemed to increase as she raced out of the bathroom into her room. "Oh my God, not now." It was like her mind was going fast, but in slow motion at the same time; her thoughts were uncontrollable, as she franticly searched through the drawers in her dresser and those feelings became more and more intense. She had suffered from anxiety for most of her life but for the last year or so she had managed to keep it under control. The events of the day had brought on a full blown attack that was only getting worst with each moment that passed without her being able to find her meds. She finally found them in the drawer of her nightstand. She raced back to the bathroom, grabbed the cup on the sink, filled it with water and popped two pills in her mouth before downing the water. Mia walked back into her room and laid her naked body on the floor at the foot of her bed. She curled herself into a ball struggling to control her thoughts as she continued crying until she fell asleep.

CHAPTER SEVEN

Bryce lay awake in the bed staring at the ceiling; he was restless. He had been trying to fall asleep for the last hour, but it felt much longer. He had been so tired after dinner, mainly due to all the ripping and running he and Tremaine had been doing all over the island with his parents. It was like since this was Tremaine's first time on vacation with them they were trying to make sure he got to see and do everything the beautiful island had to offer. Bryce understood his parents thinking because he was guilty of it too. Just in the first few hours on the island he had took his friend dirt bike riding, swimming and they had played basketball with some local kids. After eating dinner they had fallen asleep on the couch watching TV but was awakened by Mrs. Edwards and told to take a shower and to not get their "dirty behinds" in the bed until they had. They obeyed her wishes, but the shower had taken away

Bryce's sleepiness and now he was wide awake. The two friends had talked until they ran out of things to say; that was 15 minutes ago and the room was now quiet with only the sounds of the ocean filling the air. That was until Bryce's mom stuck her head in the room to check on them.

"What are you still doing up young man?" she said softly not wanting to wake up Tremaine.

"Hey ma," he said as he looked towards the beautiful middle aged woman standing in the door. "I can't fall back to sleep, so I'm just laying here listening to the ocean."

"Is everything ok, is something bothering you?" she asked as she stepped in the room and walked to the foot of his bed and sat down.

"Nooo, everything is fine, actually everything is great. I'm having so much fun. I'm glad you and dad let Tre come."

"Yeah I'm glad he is here too. You know how I feel about him, he is such a sweet boy. We all love him very much. I'm glad he is in our life. I feel like I've gained another son." she said as her voice tailed off with the thought of not actually being able to have another child.

"I know ma and he loves ya'll too. He is always talking about how much he appreciates everything that you and dad does for him."

"Well we also know how close you two are and we have become like his family, so we will continue to do all that we can to make sure he gets the things he needs."

"Thanks ma that means a lot. I love you." Bryce said with a smile.

"I love you too, now go to sleep. You need me to read you a bedtime story like when you were younger?"

"Noooo ma..."

"But you loved that remember? I'm gonna go get the 3 little bears book; that was your favorite" she said as she stood up.

"Maaaa, noooo!" Bryce said as he was now embarrassed.

Just then the sound of laughter rang out from the pallet on the floor next to the bed where Tremaine was laying and was thought to be sleep.

"Tremaine I knew you weren't sleep boy. You over there faking." Mrs. Edwards said laughing. "You been woke this whole time haven't you? And why are you sleeping on the floor in here instead of in your room?"

"Yes Ma'am I'm woke." He replied between laughs. "I'm just not used to having my own room so I couldn't sleep either." he said as he continued to laugh.

"You two take ya'll butts to bed," she said. "Before I read both of ya'll a bedtime story with my foot."

"Ok ma." Bryce who was now laughing said. "Ma, can you make your world famous banana pancakes in the morning? You know that's my favorite."

"Yes I will." Mrs. Edwards replied making her way out the door. "Goodnight."

"Goodnight!" Both boys responded.

They laughed for a few more minutes after hearing Mrs. Edwards door to her bedroom close. As the room fell silent again Tremaine said, "Banana pancakes? That does sound good, man that sound good right now."

"Yeah it does, I'm hungry again," Bryce said rubbing his stomach.

"Yeah me too."

"C'mon let's go raid the fridge" Bryce whispered as he sat up.

"Yo you think it's more of those oxtails left?" Tremaine asked.

"I don't know... only one way to find out."

"I hope so!" Tremaine exclaimed.

"You gonna get us caught. You gotta be quiet."

$$* * *$$

The blaring sound of sirens caused Mia to jump out of her sleep and sit up in her bed. Her heart was pounding and she was ready to make a dash for the door with thoughts that it may be an emergency. That was until she realized it was coming from the 42 inch flat screen across the room. Fucking Law & Order. I must've fallen asleep with the TV on again, she thought to herself as she took a deep breath and tried to slow her heart rate. Reaching for the remote on her nightstand she glanced at her phone and saw she had another 11 missed calls. "That makes 38." she said laughing to herself. It had been nearly 2 weeks since anybody had heard from her. After the stress from the trial, Bryce's crash

EAT, PREY & NO LOVE

and hospital episode she decided she needed a break from the world. So she used some much needed vacation time at work and hadn't left her house or answered her phone She rarely even opened her curtains or checked her mail; she only opened her door for food to be delivered on the nights that she decided to eat. She had run the gambit of emotions, but for some reason today felt different. She hopped up out her bed and walked across the room and opened the curtains to finally let some sun in. The glare from the bright Atlanta sun hit her face causing her to cover her eyes like the vampire she had become. "Let me call these hoes back before they put out an amber alert for me." she said as she grabbed her phone and began dialing Kim's number.

"Hello…Hello?" the voice on the other end of the phone said sounding like they were fumbling with the cellphone.

"Hey Baby, this is your Auntie Mia. Where's your mommy? Put her on the phone."

"Hi auntie, hold on ok?" the little voice said before screaming for her mother. "Maaaaaa! It's Auntie Mia on the phoooone!"

"Bring me my phone!" Kim could be heard screaming from a distance. After a few seconds Kim grabbed the phone from her daughter.

"Well it's good to know somebody's alive," she said sarcastically.

"Yeah I know I'm sorry. I just needed a break. I had so

much going on and I just needed to clear…"

"Hold on," Kim interrupted her. "Let's call Trice on 3-way so you only have to apologize and tell this story once."

"What's up girl?" Latrice said as she answered the phone. "What you up to?"

"Nothing," Kim replied. "But guess who is on the line, our missing in action former best friend."

"Bitch, where in the hell have you been? I been calling you and calling yo ass. I had Kim call the hospitals and everything. I got that bullshit text you sent letting us know you was ok, but what in the hell is up? Did you hear about Bryce's accident?" Latrice said in what seemed to be one breath.

"Yes I know all about it, I went and to see him at the hospital when it happened," an unenthused Mia replied. She was already dreading the conversation she knew she was about to have with her girls.

" You saw him!?" an excited Latrice responded waiting for the juicy gossip to start pouring out of Mia's mouth. "Well spill it bitch! What is going on? Was it really bad? Is he okay? I knew you would be the first person his ass would call. Just like a nigga! Wit they ol' trifling asses."

"Calm down Latrice! Breathe!" Kim yelled. "Let her finish! Shit let her start, before she hangs up on us. You know Mia will go back into hiding and we won't hear from her in a month of Sundays!"

"I saw him and he's fine I guess."

"You guess?" an impatient Latrice blurted.

"Yeah, what do you mean you guess?" a confused Kim asked.

"I wouldn't know since I never got to speak with him. By the time I got to the hospital he already had company. This ditsy reporter bitch was already there kissing and rubbing on him when I walked in the room."

"What!!" Both girls simultaneously yelled into the phone.

"Yes, but I really don't want to talk about it right now. I'm so not in the mood for it right now. He has obviously moved on and I am too, finally."

"Well are you gonna at least come and get that head done? 'Cause I know you looking crazy cooped up in that cave of yours," Latrice joked.

"Eventually, definitely not today though, maybe tomorrow. But as much as I would love to entertain you beautiful ladies with my ongoing drama, I'm about to take me a nice hot bath. Love ya, bye-bye!"

Mia hung up the phone and walked into the bathroom and began running the water for her bath. She wasn't quite ready to rejoin the outside world just yet but she was ready to let the outside world in. That would include letting some more sun into her gloomy condo, cleaning up and listening to some music. Pulling open the curtains in her living room allowed her to see the mess her place had become more clearly. She could see the remains of last night's Chinese food and began straightening up a little. As she walked in the kitchen she quickly remembered way she loved takeout so much, no dishes. But that thought was quickly replaced when she opened the cabinet drawer where she kept her garbage can and caught a whiff of the stench of a week and half worth of takeout in her garbage. She sprayed air fresher, but it really wasn't doing anything to hide the smell. She heard a knock at the door just as she closed the drawer. She wasn't expecting company and she definitely wasn't the just drop by type. She walked to the door and looked through the peephole to see who it was but was greeted by what looked to be 3 dozen of roses.

"Who is it?" Mia shouted.

"Delivery." replied the person on the other side of the door. "Delivery for a Ms. Mia Armstrong."

"One second please," Mia said as she closed her robe and tied it up. She thought to herself how this was a typical Bryce move. He thought roses and his smile could cure all. Not this time though, not with her, not anymore.

"Listen I'm sorry for the inconvenience of you having to come all the way over here, but I would greatly appreciate if you would return those to sender," she said as she swung open the door with an attitude.

"Sorry ma'am but I don't think that's possible," the

delivery man said.

"And why is that?" Mia asked.

"Because why you don't want my roses for?" the man said in a goofy voice as he lowered the roses revealing his face.

"Christion?" Mia said with a look of shock on her face. "What are you doing here and how did you find out where I live?"

"I'm a lawyer it's my job to find out things," he charmingly said with a smile on his face.

"I'm gonna kill Angela," Mia said causing him to laugh as she quickly realized where he had received his info.

"You'd be surprised what buying lunch all week will get you, that plus begging," he said honestly. "I was worried about you though. Last time I saw you was that night at the hospital. No matter what you said you didn't look like everything was ok. Then I hadn't seen you at work, so I just was a little concerned."

"Well I appreciate your concern. I really do but to be honest with you I'm really not in the mood for company and to be even more truthful I really don't like people dropping by unannounced."

"I understand, and it's not a problem. I really just wanted to make sure you..."

"Oh my God!" Mia suddenly shouted as she took off running towards the bathroom in her room remembering the water she had running for her bath. Christion stood at the door confused not knowing what was happening. He didn't know whether to stand there holding the roses or put them down and leave. He decided to stand there holding them until he heard a scream come from the direction Mia had ran. He stepped in and put the roses down on the first table he saw and headed in that direction.

"Mia," he called out as he walked down the hall.

"I'm in here," she replied.

Christion made his way through Mia's room into the bathroom where he saw her standing in a pool of water from the over flowing tub. "Oh shit," he blurted out as he saw what all the panic was about.

"You gotta bathing suit?" he joked trying to lighten up the mood.

"A what?" Mia snarled clearly not getting the joke.

"Where do you keep your towels?" Christion asked as he rolled up his pant legs.

Mia pointed to the linen closet. Christion walked over to the closet and began to grab as many towels as he could. As he stepped into the bathroom and reached out to hand Mia a few towels, he lost his footing on the slick floor and fell onto his back causing him to burst into laughter. Mia immediately burst out laughing as well. She made her way towards him to help him up and began losing her footing too and fell right on top of him causing both of them to bust out laughing again.

"I call myself coming to the rescue and now I need rescuing," Christion said between laughs.

"Yeah, some hero," Mia joked.

"Are you entertained?" he replied with a smile. "Glad I can provide you with some laughter."

"Much needed laughter to be honest." Mia answered before she had even realized she said it. But she was telling the truth; it was actually the first time she had smiled or laughed in a while. They laid there laughing for a moment before an awkward silence filled the room as they both realized the position they were in. All of a sudden they both tried getting up, only to fall down again in the same position. Mia laid her head on his chest and laughed uncontrollably until she almost couldn't breathe. Christion placed his hand on top of Mia's head and began stroking her hair as they lay laughing trying to catch their breath. Christion looked down at the beautiful woman lying on top of him and noticed that her wet hair was in her face and decided to remove it while caressing the side of her face. The gesture caught Mia off guard, but as she looked up at him and they made eye contact she realized that she didn't mind it. She actually liked it. His touch was gentle and soothing and she had been through so much lately the thought of indulging in some pleasure made her body temperature start to rise. But just as fast as the thought entered her mind, it exited. Christion was gorgeous, even better looking than Bryce. He was extremely sexy and from where Mia was laying she could feel that he was blessed as well. But he was her co-worker, which meant he was totally off limits even if it was just for a quick rumble in the sheets. But the more she felt the bulge in his pants increase the more she felt herself not wanting to resist. She tried to get up hoping that putting a little space between the two of them would stop the juices beginning to flow between her legs. But as she did Christion put his arms around her and pulled her back to him. Christion gripped the back of Mia's head and passionately placed his full lips against hers. With no resistance Mia received his soft tongue in her mouth and welcomed it with hers. Feeling all sorts of vibrations flowing through her body she began grinding up against his dick. He was fully erect now; she could almost feel it throbbing against her pelvic area. Mia couldn't take it anymore. Her interest was at its peak and she had to feel it. She unbuttoned his pants exposing his rock hard penis and began stroking his massive manhood. As Mia's hand went up and down on his dick, Christion's body began moving in rhythm with every stroke, showing her that he was enjoying it. Mia rose to her feet and dropped her robe revealing her pink laced Victoria Secret panties and bra. Christion was even more turned on at the sight of the sexy woman standing over top of him.

"Got damn you sexy."

"Shhh…don't talk," Mia said as she dropped her panties and mounted him. Just like in the courtroom she was in control as she bounced up and down on his dick like a pogo stick. As she felt herself about to cum she grabbed both his hands and made him put them on her ass and squeeze, which made her explode all over his dick. Christion quickly flipped her over onto her back and began to loosen her bra straps exposing her perky hershey kiss nipples. He sucked on each perky breast and she gyrated her hips against him letting him know she was enjoying every bit of it. He worked his way from her breast down to her stomach, licking and sucking not missing a spot. Christion made his way down to her pussy and with no surprise her legs were spread wide open. Her clean shaven vagina patiently waited for what it was about to receive. He started sucking on her sweet nectar as if his life depended on it and she showed her gratitude by palming the back of his head and suffocating his face with her now glistening pussy. She moaned for more, exciting Christion and causing him to suck on her clit harder and harder until she let out an orgasmic scream and her juices flowed on his tongue and down his throat. Her moans grew louder as he pinned her hands down and entered her soaking wet vagina. Mia's eyes widened with pleasure and pain by the thickness and length that just took over her tight wet walls. Seeing the look on her face Christion told her, "I'll stop if you want me to." Mia never replied; instead she wrapped her legs around his waist and welcomed every thrust he gave her by digging her manicured nails into his back. He could feel himself reaching his climax and began to pump harder, causing Mia's climax to build as well until they both exploded on each other. Christion rolled over onto his back and laid next to Mia and tried to catch his breath as the room fell silent. After a few minutes had passed he decided to break the silence.

"Awkward," he blurted out slowly for the effect hoping to get a response of some sort.

Mia, however, had so many thoughts racing through her mind she was unable to provide a response.

"Ooook…" Christion said aloud. "Guess this is the part where I put my clothes on and leave, huh?" he said jokingly waiting for a reaction.

Still nothing, Mia just laid there looking like a woman full of regret. Just as Christion had decided to get up and put his clothes back on Mia stood up and began walking her naked self towards her bedroom. She didn't say a word until she reached the bathroom door. That's when she looked over her shoulder back at him lying there on the floor confused and seductively.

"Are you coming or what?"

Christion's eyes lit up as he attempted to jump up off the floor only to lose his balance once again on the slippery surface. "Oh, for sure!" he said regaining his balance before following her into her bedroom, dick first.

CHAPTER EIGHT

The October weather had begun to set in and was doing its part to cool off the city of Atlanta. But it seemed to only heat up the chemistry between Mia and Christion. Ever since their hot and steamy encounter at Mia's they had been involved in a sexual relationship. That had included late night rendezvous at different hotels throughout the city and a few weekend getaways. They had managed to keep their sexual relationship a secret from everyone at the office, as well as Mia's two best friends. They enjoyed the fact that no one knew a thing. They would get a kick out of company meetings in the conference room, knowing that the night before they had been on top of that same table having great sex. Mia, without getting into too many details, expressed that she was not looking to get in a relationship so feelings would need to be left at the door. Christion agreed and decided that he wouldn't ask too many questions, allowing Mia to open up to him at her own leisure. But he was keeping a secret. Out of respect for her he didn't mind all the sneaking around, but lately those feelings that were supposed to be checked at the door had begun to creep in. He really admired Mia: her strength, her drive, her focus and of course her beauty. He had since his earliest days at the firm. It was why he dropped by her office to ask so many questions, most of the time he already knew the answer. It was why he showed up to court that day to watch her in action. She was definitely his type of woman, the type of woman he could see himself having a future with. A future that at one time didn't seem possible growing up on the drug infested streets of Harlem.

Christion Bradshaw was raised by his maternal grandmother after his mother was sent to prison for her involvement in an armed robbery turned shooting at a popular clothing store in the Bronx. She eventually died in prison before being released due to the HIV virus she had contracted by sharing needles or prostituting to support her heroin addiction. That left Christion living with his grandmother full time. His grandmother tried to do everything she could to protect him from the traps and pitfalls of the street that had claimed so many young lives before him. But her best efforts couldn't shield him from what he saw right outside his window of their project apartment. Hand to hand drug deals, fist fights that led to shoot outs, fancy cars, and fast women. The allure of the streets was too much for most kids his age to resist. But he was determined not to fall victim. He wanted out of the projects and he knew education was his way out. So he hit the books hard and earned a scholarship to NYU where he studied law. He excelled and graduated near the top of his class before passing the bar and joining one of the best law firms in New York. Being a bright young lawyer at a top firm afforded him luxuries that he had always dreamed of. The main one was buying his grandmother a house in her hometown of Atlanta. That was why he had decided to move down there to be with her after she had fallen ill. It was why he spent most of his time outside of work right here, sitting in the same chair next to her bedside in her hospital room. He would spend hours talking to her about the things going on in his life; mostly it was work related but as of late "the thing" with Mia, for lack of a better term, had been the topic.

He was able to tell his grandmother about the strong feelings that had begun to develop for her. Feelings he had to suppress due to not only the secret nature of their relationship but also because he could tell Mia had been scarred in a previous relationship. Deeply scarred he speculated but wasn't sure because that, like a lot of things with Mia, was off limits. He wished she would open up to him; he wanted to know more of her, not just her body. He wanted to learn about the hurt and heartaches and he wanted to be part of her healing process. But it was almost like she locked her emotions in a box and buried them in a place only she knew. She was definitely in control and he was playing by her rules. Playing by someone else's rules in a relationship was something he was not used to. He was usually the one making and breaking the rules. Christion had been blessed with extremely good looks and he could easily pass for a model. Most women leaped at the chance to be with him and would do almost anything for him. He had been caught cheating on many of them, only to be easily forgiven and welcomed back in their hearts and beds. He had slept with sets of friends after not being able to decide which ones he wanted more and had his share of threesomes. But a lot of those things were done by a young and immature Christion. That was his past. He had been hoping and looking for something more serious, but he wanted a challenge. A woman who wouldn't just give into his charm and good looks. A woman with character who knew exactly what she wanted and knew where she was going in life. That was what he saw in Mia and what he had been expressing to his grandmother for the past hour. It wasn't until the nurse knocked on the door to tell him that visiting hours were about to end that he realized that he had been talking about Mia the whole time. He needed to leave anyway he hadn't intended to stay that long. He stood up and kissed his grandmother on the forehead, wishing they had more time; but more than that he wished she could join in on the one way conversations he would have with her as she laid there, silent, in a comatose state. In his heart he knew that would never happen. She was losing her fight with brain cancer and most likely she would never wake up again. But that wouldn't stop him for coming to talk with the woman who meant so much to him.

Christion's phone began to beep as soon as he stepped out of the hospital. He didn't have reception inside the hospital so all his messages began flooding his phone at the same time. Without even looking he already had an idea who they were from.

Where are u? U should be here already.

We should be on the road by now.

Christion shook his head knowing how demanding Mia could be. Being on her bad side was not somewhere most people wanted to be. He dialed her number and prepared for the wrath.

"Where the hell are you at?" she said as soon as she picked up.

"I'm on my way right now."

"Where have you been Christion? We were supposed be gone already," she said with anger in her voice.

"I'll explain to you when I get there. I'll be there in 10

minutes."

"Whatever," she said before hanging up.

Christion pulled his black 745 into the parking garage beneath Mia's building. He could feel her eyes burning a hole through the window of his car as she stood in front of the elevator with her bags. He knew he would have some making up to do on their ride to the cabin he had rented in the mountains of North Georgia. He parked and hopped out to help her with her bags. She handed him the bags and opened the passenger door and got in without saying a word to him. Christion smirked as he put her bags in the trunk. He was kind of turned on by her attitude. He knew she was just putting on. If she had been that mad she wouldn't have been downstairs waiting when he arrived.

They had been riding for what seemed like a half hour before Mia decided to say something. Christion had been counting down the time waiting for her to voice her displeasure with his lateness.

"So," she said whipping her body around in her seat to look at him.

"Soooo, what?" Christion replied slowly.

"You said you would explain yourself when you picked me up. So...I'm waiting," Mia said sarcastically.

"Well first of all I would really like to apologize, but I had a very good reason."

"Oh really?" Mia asked looking suspicious. "I can't wait

to hear this one."

"Well since we were gonna be away for the entire weekend, I wanted to stop by and check on my grandmother before I left. I needed to speak with her doctors and I ended up being there a lot longer than I planned," Christion said before looking over at Mia. "But once again I am truly sorry for keeping YOU waiting."

Mia immediately began feeling bad. Here she was acting like a diva and Christion was only trying to make sure his grandmother was situated before he went out of town. Who cares if he was a little late. He was doing exactly what he was supposed to do, and the more she thought about how she was acting the worse she felt.

"I'm sorry," she said as she put her hand on the back of his head and began rubbing it. "Why didn't you just say so?" she asked.

"I know how women can be when they are mad. I figured I'd let you calm down a little."

"Am I really that bad?" she asked slightly embarrassed.

Christion grabbed her hand and kissed it before jokingly saying, "Yes."

The hour and a half drive up the highway seemed like it went by fast with the two of them sharing laughs and swapping stories. Mia hadn't even noticed they had gotten there so fast until she saw Christion pull up in front of the extra-large Cypress log home just off Highway 17. Mia stepped out of the car and took in her surroundings. The view from the mountain top getaway was beautiful. Mia walked onto the wrap around porch and made her way around the side and to the back of the house. She immediately noticed the outdoor fireplace on the back porch along with the large outdoor Jacuzzi. She thought to herself how she would definitely be putting both of those to use sometime that weekend along with a bottle of her favorite wine. She stood on the back porch soaking in the long range view; lost in deep thought she didn't notice Christion coming out of the backdoor onto the porch. He startled her slightly as he wrapped his arms around her waist and kissed her on her neck.

"You like it?" he asked.

"I love it, this is beautiful Christion," she responded. "Do you know I've lived in Georgia all of my life and I've never been up here before. I'm always leaving the state for a vacation— but look at all of this, who would've known."

"Yeah, sometimes you can go looking for something only to find out it's been right in front of you the whole time," he whispered as he started nibbling on her ear. Mia began to grind on him as she felt his dick on her ass. "Come on let's go see the rest of the house." Christion said stopping himself. He didn't want to ruin his plans. This weekend wasn't about sex even though he was sure they were going to have plenty of it. It was about sweeping Mia off her feet and getting her to let him in. He wanted to show her that she could trust him with her heart.

* * *

"That was good," Mia said as she looked down at her empty plate. "Where did you learn to cook like that?"

"You ain't know I could put it down like that huh?" Christion said bragging. "Grams always said a woman loves a man who can cook, so she had me in the kitchen early in the game."

"Well, she taught you well," Mia said smiling.

Christion had pulled out all the stops: char-grilling salmon and topping it with shrimp, lobster meat, mushrooms and spinach in a Monterey cheese sauce over yellow rice. He lit the outdoor fireplace and served her a romantic candlelight dinner on the back porch taking full advantage of the beautiful mountain top view. But he wasn't done, he had something else up his sleeve.

"I hope you saved some room for dessert."

"Dessert? Boy stop," Mia said cutting her eyes at him.

"No I'm for real but first I need you to go upstairs in the room and look on the bed."

"What!?" Mia said clearly not wanting to move.

"Trust me you are gonna like it," he said flashing his irresistible smile.

Mia made her way up the steps and into the master

EAT, PREY & NO LOVE

bedroom of the cabin. In the middle of the king sized bed sat a red gift box with a white bowed ribbon. Mia sat on the bed and read the note attached to the box.

Put this on, then come join me for dessert.

She untied the bow and opened the box. Inside the box was a black Flirtatious ribbons & lace apron and matching black mesh panties from Fredrick's of Hollywood.

Christion watched as Mia descended the steps looking like a sexy housemaid. She looked exactly how he had pictured she would when he picked out the ultra-sexy lingerie set. He had turned off all the lights downstairs but the fire burning in the fireplace was all the light they would need. The sound of her pink Christian Louboutin pumps clicking across the wood floor as she made her way towards him was like music to his ears. Once she was close enough for the light to hit her fully, he could feel his manhood begin to rise. Mia was turning him on and she knew it. She did a spin so he could get the full view of what she looked like in the gift he had purchased for her.

"You like?" she seductively asked already knowing the answer. She looked good and she knew it. She had double checked while touching up her make-up in the mirror upstairs. The black fabric looked good against her skin and the pumps she had on seemed to make her fat ass poke out even more than normal.

"Definitely," Christion quickly responded. "You ready

for some dessert?"

Mia looked down seeing the layout he had prepared for them: freshly sliced strawberries, chocolate dipping sauce and a bottle of Perrier Jouet Rosé sitting in a bucket of ice. She liked it already as she took a seat joining him on the rug in front of the fireplace. Christion popped the bottle of champagne and filled the two glasses before passing her one.

"Are you enjoying yourself?" he asked.

"Yes," she answered. "It's a little different for us but..."

"But what?" he questioned.

"But different isn't a bad thing, it's actually good in our case." She said revealing the first crack in the wall she had built between them.

"That's good, it should feel different. To be honest it feels right," he said as he grabbed a strawberry, dipped it in chocolate, and fed it to her.

Mia bit the strawberry to keep from answering, but inside she agreed with him. It did feel right being around him. She started to feel flutters lately when she saw him around the office. She even noticed herself feeling jealous when she would see the female receptionist flirt with him every day. What had started out as a no strings attached fun thing for her had slowly become something she found herself wanting more of. She didn't know if she was ready to admit it to him or herself, remembering she was the one who had laid the ground rules for their relationship. But her feelings for him had definitely changed. Christion had given her the space she needed while still being there and even though she ran hot and cold with him, he remained the same. Little did she know Christion shared the same feelings of wanting to make something more of their relationship.

"Mia I know you've been hurt in you past, the depths of which I don't know. But I'm willing to be the one to help you get past that. I wanna be the one to restore your faith in men and in love."

"Christion I'm really not..."

"Just hear me out," he continued. "I feel it when you are around me. I feel you fighting against yourself denying the obvious. Why continue to fight it? Allow yourself to be happy. Whoever the person is responsible for your hurt has probably moved on with their life and I bet they are enjoying their happiness. But you won't allow yourself to do the same. That's not fair to you. You owe yourself better than that."

Mia felt the tears in the wells of her eyes began to fill. She knew what he had just said was right. She felt like she had been stripped naked emotionally and she was now standing there with all of her flaws showing. Flaws she tried her best to hide. Tears began to run down her face as she could no longer hide from her truth. She had fallen in love with the wrong man and she was punishing herself for his mistakes.

Seeing her tears, Christion felt like he had maybe went

too far, maybe he had been too hard on her. He never meant to hurt her feelings. He was actually trying to do the exact opposite. He only wanted to give her confidence to trust and love again. He wiped the tears running down her face.

"I'm sorry I wasn't trying to…"

"No it's ok," she said interrupting him. "You're right, you're 100% right. I have to start living for me again."

"Right, it's ok to be a lil' selfish when it comes to your happiness. Matter of fact let's drink to that. To happiness!" he said as he raised his glass trying to lighten the mood.

"To happiness." Mia repeated as she lifted her glass before taking a sip. She grabbed a strawberry, dipped it in chocolate, bit it then fed the rest to him. She enjoyed it as Christion slowly sucked the juices off her fingers.

"You know what would make me happy right now?" she asked with sexiness dripping from every word.

"What's that?"

"If you were to come over here and eat this strawberry," she replied as she laid back and spread her legs and started rubbing on her clit through her panties.

Christion was more than willing to oblige. He removed her panties and dived face first into her sweet spot. The warmth of his tongue on her clit caused her to grab the back of his head as she grounded her pussy in his face. She could feel her clit beginning to swell as he alternated licking it and sucking it hard. He knew that drove her crazy and the harder he sucked the more she grinded. Christion ate her pussy like he had never done before. She was on the verge of an orgasm. She laid her head back, closed her eyes while biting her bottom lip and let his mouth take her to ecstasy. She let out a loud moan letting him know that he had gotten her there. Christion was so hard that his dick was throbbing, he felt like his dick had a heartbeat. Mia sat up, the sight of the massive bulge in his pants making her mouth water. She unzipped his pants and quickly took him into her mouth. She was giving him some of the wettest and sloppiest head he had ever received. He knew if she continued that he wouldn't be able to last much longer. He didn't want to cum yet; he wanted to feel her juice box on his dick. He stopped her from sucking his dick and turned her around. Mia exploded as soon as Christion entered her from behind. He felt so good inside of her. All you could hear was her fat ass slapping against him as she went back and forth on his rock hard pole. He gripped her ass cheeks with both hands and began pumping harder and harder as he felt himself about to climax.

"I'm about to cum!" he yelled. Mia gripped the rug for leverage and began bouncing her ass back on him even faster. He quickly pulled out and starting cumming all over her ass before they both collapsed. As they laid there cuddling naked in front of the fireplace, Mia thought to herself, Damn he just fucked the shit outta me. I'm gonna cook his ass a big breakfast in the morning, just before she closed her eyes and drifted off to sleep.

CHAPTER NINE

"We are running out of time! I need these to be over there. It's not rocket science people!" Eva shouted, as she directed the workers preparing Bryce's home for his birthday party. Her original plans for his party had to be scrapped after his accident. She tried to convince him to cancel the party all together, but he insisted on it happening. So she was forced to come up with a new idea on the fly and she was now praying it all came together. "Faster, faster!" she continued yelling. She looked down at her phone checking the time and began pacing back and forth as she dialed a number.

Bryce leaned against the doorway watching as his best friend talked on the phone while continuing to direct traffic. She was the queen of multi-tasking; if she hadn't been the best event planner in Atlanta he would've welcomed her with open arms at his company. He knew she was in go mode and like usual he decided to mess with her a bit.

"So how's everything going?" he asked clearly seeing the chaos.

"How's everything going?" she asked as she turned seeing him. "How does it look like it's going? I got lights in the wrong place, only half of the alcohol got delivered and my chef and servers are stuck in traffic. You know I don't work like this Bryce. But you had to have your party. Look at you, you're not even completely healed." She said pointing to the cane he was holding in his hand.

"I'm fine Eva and for the record you're doing a wonderful job. It will all come together, it always does. You're the best in the business remember," he said as he turned and walked away.

Bryce's home had been transformed into the perfect setting for the masquerade themed party. As usual he spared no expense to making sure his guests would enjoy themselves. It started as soon as the black Maybachs he had arranged to pick them up pulled up. Guests stepped out of the luxury vehicles onto a red carpet as photographers snapped pictures of them, making each guest feel like a star. They were then escorted into the large ballroom decorated in white and gold. Tables lined both sides of the room creating a natural dance floor and were equally as elegant as the room's décor, matching the white and gold theme. Every high end fashion designer was represented throughout the room with both men and women alike looking their very best.

Bryce and Marcus stood at the top of the white spiral staircase looking down at all the masked party goers, sharing a drink as they admired the job that Eva had done.

"I can't believe Eva was able to pull this shit off," Marcus stated between sips of his drink.

"Yeah, she did her thing. The place looks great. You should've seen this shit a few hours ago, she had me nervous." Bryce explained.

"Come on let's get down here and enjoy the festivities," Marcus said as he put his drink down. "You need some help bruh?"

"Nah, I'm good," Bryce said as he put his hand on the railing and used his cane for stability and made his way down the steps trying to disguise his discomfort.

Bryce gingerly made his way through the party greeting people, shaking hands and thanking attendees for coming. He was finally able to introduce Marcus to Natasha Cozier— who he had flown in on his private jet as one of his special invited guest. She wore a sexy red dress with a matching Cecilia mask on a stick. Marcus, like every other man in the room, couldn't keep his eyes off her for the rest of the night.

Bryce spent the early part of the night sitting at his table watching everyone else party. Everyone from Eva to Marcus to Yolanda, even Kim and her husband took turns sitting at his table talking with him throughout the night. He was currently watching the person who had spent the most time with him during the night. Erica was working the room in a black dress and a silver Josephine mask. Her tight fitting dress could barely contain her thick voluptuous figure and Bryce couldn't help but to admire and smirk as he thought about peeling her out of it later on that night. Bryce, while not exclusive, had begun to spend more time with her as of late. After his accident Erica had become somewhat of a consistent presence in his life by making it her business to be there for him in any way possible. She was slowly positioning herself to be more than just a friend and made no secret of her desires. Bryce, on the other hand, wanted no parts of another serious relationship at the moment although he enjoyed the time they spent together. He continued to scan the room, taking in all the sexy women in attendance. His eyes landed on a woman in a even sexier black dress who had just entered the room holding a mysterious white mask with a hand painted black design accented with diamonds over her face. His world seemed to stand still for a moment. He found himself staring, unable to turn away as the mystery woman made her way towards the bar. Her confident strut, track star body and beautiful brown complexion had captured his attention and rang so familiar to him. Bryce rose from his seat still not believing his eyes, it had been months since he last seen her and wasn't sure if she'd even show up.

"She showed up," he whispered to himself making his way across the room unable to move as fast as he would've liked. "Mia?" he asked finally reaching the woman standing at the bar with her back to him.

"Hello Bryce," she replied as she turned and lowered her mask revealing her beautiful face and piercing eyes.

"It's really nice to see you Mia"

"It's nice to be seen," she stated coldly while grabbing a hors d'oeuvres off the tray of a passing server.

"I didn't know if you would come or not, but I'm really happy you decided to," he said smiling, hoping to thaw the icy stare she was giving him.

"Oh I wouldn't miss this for the world," she replied finally cracking a smile.

"I wasn't sure after how things ended with us. I never really got a chance to explain..."

"No explanation needed," she said cutting him short as her smile widened.

It was then that Bryce realized that she had not been smiling at him at all. Truth was she hadn't even been looking at him. Her smile was reserved for the person standing just a few feet behind Bryce.

"Sorry babe, I had left my phone in the car," Christion said as he stepped around Bryce, placing his arm around Mia's waist and kissed her on the cheek. "Who's this babe?" he said, noticing the man standing in front of them.

"Christion this is Bryce, Bryce this is Christion," Mia replied.

"Hey, how you doing?" Christion said extending his hand.

He couldn't believe the audacity she had bringing her new man to his party. What the fuck? She must be outta her fucking mind bringing this nigga here. What kind of bullshit games she playin'. This bitch crazy, he thought to himself. In his eyes she had definitely went too far this time.

"What's up," he said breaking the brief moment of silence, but not returning the gesture all while never breaking eye contact with Mia. He was burning up with rage on the inside as he took in the scene unfolding in front of him.

Marcus seen the unfamiliar look on his friend's face and immediately knew he needed to intervene. It wasn't like Bryce to cause a scene, but Marcus also knew that when egos and women are involved things could go left fast. He walked up on the three of them and tried to break the tension.

"Miaaa!" he shouted reaching out hugging her. "Who's your date?" he asked releasing her from his embrace.

"Hi Marcus, this is Christion, my boyfriend." She said

sending another dig at Bryce.

"Christion huh, oh ok, what's up?" Marcus said shaking his still extended hand. "Nice mask."

"Mia can I speak with you for a minute, solo?" Bryce chimed in ignoring Marcus's attempt at small talk.

"Not a…"

"Actually Eva sent me over here to get you bruh. She needs you over there." Marcus said before she could answer.

Bryce reluctantly made his way back to the other side of the room with Marcus closely following. "Man you saw that shit? She brought some ol' random nigga to my party, to my house," he said anger oozing off of every word.

"Yeah she outta bounds on that one. But tonight's not the night… let her have that one. It's your born day bruh let's get fucked up."

Mia watched as Bryce and Marcus disappeared into the crowd. She hadn't been completely honest with Christion about whose party they were attending. She didn't want to take the chance of him not wanting to go if he knew the truth. She really wanted to see the look on Bryce's face when she walked in with Christion on her arm. She knew it was wrong but it felt right. Bryce had to know that he wasn't the only game in town and she needed to show him first hand.

"What was that about?" Christion asked clearly noticing the tension between her and Bryce.

"What?" she replied. Christion had caught her off guard.

"Oh, nothing that's Bryce; this is his party."

"Yeah? Ok, but I was talking about that tension in the air."

"You noticed that huh?" Mia said knowing she had to come clean. "Bryce is my ex Christion."

"Your ex…" Christion stated slowly letting it sink in.

"Yes, my ex fiancé."

"Really?"

"I know it was wrong to bring you here and I'm sorry…"

"So Bryce Edwards is your ex and you brought me to his birthday party?" he said chuckling.

"I don't know what I was thinking. We can just leave, come on let's leave."

"Leave?" he asked. "For what? So he can see you run out of here looking weak. Not gonna happen. Not while you're with me. You're my woman now. You brought me to your ex's party, so what. I wish you would've put me on to your lil' plan but I understand. You wanna rub it in his face, I'm wit that. Let's hit this dance floor and give em a show."

"You for real?" Mia said not believing her ears and how well he took her news. She was so turned on by him at that moment. She couldn't believe how much she had underestimated him.

"Yeah, I got you come on."

The party was in full swing. The DJ had everybody on the dance floor playing hit record after hit record. Although young black America's high society was fully represented, nobody was acting high siddity. This was apparent by the reaction when the DJ played French Montana's new record. Businessmen, high powered execs, lawyers: both men and women all sang the chorus in unison. Marcus stood next to Bryce rapping along in between sips from the bottle of Luc Belaire Rare Rose in his hand.

"Nigga it's some bad bitches in here," he said.

Bryce just nodded his head in agreement. He honestly hadn't been able to pay attention to any of the beautiful assortment of women there celebrating his birthday. He had been preoccupied watching Mia laugh and dance with Christion all night. The anger he felt seemed to only increase with each sip of the drink in his hand. He was no longer able to sit idle and not say anything. Mia had really played herself with her latest move and he felt the need to let her know just that. Bryce put his now empty drink down and without saying a word to Marcus began walking over towards Mia, who along with Christion, was standing talking with another couple.

"Mia can I talk to you for a minute?" Bryce said interrupting the group conversation.

"No not right now Bryce," Mia said clearly annoyed. "Can't you see I'm talking?"

"Can't you see I don't care?" Bryce said slightly raising his voice causing Christion to intervene.

"The lady said she don't wanna talk."

"Who the fuck asked you?"

"Ain't nobody gotta ask when it comes to mine. You feel me?" Christion said stepping between Mia and Bryce.

"What?!" Bryce said stepping into Christion face.

Mia, seeing things were about to get out of hand, stepped between the two men trying to cool the tension before other party goers could notice. "No Christion, I got this," she said putting her hand on his chest. "Bryce are you drunk or something? What is wrong with you?"

"What's wrong with me?" Bryce said looking at her like she had two heads. "You really asking me that? Take a walk with me real quick. Let me holla at you. I'm not trying to put all these people in my business."

After a quick moment of silence Mia looked over at Christion, who nodded his head showing he was okay with it, before agreeing to speak with Bryce privately. Bryce laughed as he turned to walk away at Mia needing Christion's approval.

"I'll be right back, then we can leave," Mia said before following behind Bryce.

Bryce made his way down one of the hallways in his massive home away from all the noise into a room that housed a large pool table and a well-stocked bar. Mia, only a few steps behind, entered the room that was so familiar to her. They had spent many nights drinking and playing strip pool there, which led to lots of sex on top of the very pool table she was now leaning against.

"Yo Mia, what the fuck were you thinking bringing the next nigga to my house...to my party? Are you outta ya mind?" Bryce asked clearly upset by her antics.

"You started this game with your news reporter bitch and lord knows how many other bitches. Your shit is sloppy. I'm hearing you sporting this whack bitch all over town."

"It ain't even like that, but I don't owe you no explanation after this shit you pulled. You took it to a whole other level of disrespect. You ain't never gotta worry about a nigga like me fucking wit you ever again."

"As if you had a chance nigga. I'm not these other bitches Bryce. I'm not impressed by you. I don't need you for shit and I never have. You love these sideline hoes out here lining up to suck your dick, hoping you take em on a shopping spree or fly them somewhere. You like that shit, you can't handle being with a strong bitch like me. That's why ya pussy ass backed out on getting married."

"Who the fuck you think you talking to?" Bryce yelled.

"You!" Mia yelled back tears falling from her eyes. She was finally letting it all out. All of her hurt was spilling out like venom. "Fuck you Bryce, I put up with your shit for too long. Disrespect? How dare you, you don't know disrespect until the news of your engagement being called off is in the newspaper before you can tell your family and friends.

Disrespect? How about you flying strippers all over the place."

Bryce didn't care about all her hurt and tears at the moment, only the fact that she had tried to embarrass him at his own party. What she was saying held no weight to him and neither did she. "Mia just go back out there and get your boyfriend and both of yall get the fuck out my house."

"Fuck you!" Mia said as she walked out the door leaving Bryce alone in the room.

Bryce picked up the cue ball from the pool table and threw it across the room. He had always hoped that Mia would show up, that's why he insisted on making sure Eva sent her an invitation to her job as well as her home. But he was now second guessing that choice. Her mere presence had ruined his evening and he was no longer in a partying mood. Still he wasn't about to ruin everybody else's good time or all the hard work that Eva did, so he decided he would retire to his room and crash. No singing happy birthday, no cake— no nothing. He turned the light off and walked out the room towards the steps that led upstairs to the master bedroom. As he got to the bottom of the steps he heard a noise and seen a light coming from the room where his office was, causing him to stop in his tracks. People attending the party weren't allowed access to that part of the house so no one should be remotely close to his home office. Bryce immediately changed directions, heading straight for where the light and noise were coming from. When he reached the room, the door was slightly cracked. He could see what looked to be a man in a suit rummaging through the drawers of the desk as well as the papers on top of the desk. Bryce couldn't get a good look of the man because like all the other party attendants he had a mask covering his face. Bryce pushed the door open catching the intruder by surprise.

"Yo what the hell are you doing in here!?" Bryce said startling the man.

Seeing Bryce, the man looked around the room for a way to escape, quickly realizing that his only way out was through the same door he came in— the same door Bryce was now blocking.

"How the hell you get in here?" Bryce asked trying to get a response hoping he could recognize the voice.

The man remained silent only moving closer towards a still injured Bryce who tried to raise his cane and swing it like a bat to no avail. His sore ribs wouldn't allow him to move as swift as he would've like and the man quickly rushed him knocking him to the floor. His cane fell out of his hand and the man picked it up and struck him with it a few times making sure he stayed down. The man then dropped the cane and ran out of the room.

Bryce staggered to his feet and out into the hallway holding onto the wall for balance. He was dizzy and could feel the warmth from the blood running down his face. His ribs felt like they had been broken again as they throbbed in pain. Erica had come looking for him after he had disappeared from the party and she ran down the hallway to him as she saw him struggling to walk. He collapsed into her arms as soon as she reached him. She began screaming for help when she saw the blood leaking from the cut on his head.

CHAPTER TEN

Kim yelled for her husband to get the door as she heard the door bell ringing from the kitchen. She had planned this dinner night for everyone to formally meet Mia's new man. She told everyone to be there by 7 p.m. and like clockwork Mia was on time and like usual Latrice had called to say she was running a little late. Kim was the classic stay at home wife and mother. Her husband, Rodney, owned a towing company and provided a good living for their family. She enjoyed running her household, helping her daughter, Lyric, with her schoolwork and taking her to gymnastics. She also enjoyed potty training her younger son RJ. But the thing she loved most was cooking and everybody loved her cooking. Kim's family was originally from New Orleans and although she was raised in Atlanta, she maintained those Creole roots when it came to the kitchen. Tonight she was making her famous seafood gumbo.

"Girl you got it smelling like Pappadeux's in here." Mia said as she walked in the kitchen.

"Now you know better, Pappadeux's ain't got nothing on me," Kim bragged truthfully. "I'm glad you're here though, you can start the margaritas."

"Ok, no problem. Where is Ms. LaTrice?" Mia asked while washing her hands.

"Late like always," Kim answered. "So we haven't really had a chance to talk since the party."

"Yeah."

"That was an interesting place to announce your new relationship."

"Yeah I know but…"

"I'm not judging. I'm your girl at the end of the day. Ride or die. I just don't want you jumping back into something too fast or as a get back at Bryce, you know?"

"Yeah I understand your concerns Mother Goose, but it's not about Bryce anymore; it's all about my happiness. And that episode at the party was a little self- gratification," Mia said with a smile just as the guys walked in.

"Hey Christion, nice seeing you again," Kim said.

"Hey Kim, it's nice seeing you too. You have a beautiful home," Christion said.

"Rod, grab me some glasses for these Mia-ritas," Mia

said jokingly causing everyone to laugh.

Their good time was interrupted by the sound of the doorbell signaling Latrice's arrival.

"I got it babe," Rodney said.

"Heeeeey everybody!" LaTrice said as she entered the kitchen holding two bottles of Ciroc in her hand. " Everybody this is Brinks," she said introducing the light skinned gentleman sporting the low cut with tattoos up and down his arms, who had entered the room behind her. Obviously, to everybody in the room, he was part of her baller of the month club.

Brinks spoke to everyone in the room then paused when his eyes landed on Christion. Christion noticed the inquisitive look the stranger gave him, but before he could say anything Brinks asked him a question.

"Don't I know you from somewhere?"

"From where?" Christion asked.

"I don't know but your face look familiar," the hustler asked as he rubbed his chin hoping it would jog his memory.

"I'm not from Atlanta..." Christion proclaimed.

"Me neither, I'm from New York," Brinks informed him.

"Oh ok, me too. I can't place your face either, but it's a big city. So you never know." Christion replied.

"Drinks are ready!" Mia shouted from the other side of the kitchen, shifting everyone's attention to the big pitcher in her hands.

"Good 'cause I need a drink." Latrice exclaimed with excitement.

* * *

The light coming from Bryce's office slightly illuminated the darkened hallway of the deserted office building. The Phoenix project had fallen behind schedule with all the turmoil that had been going on in Bryce's life and his investors had begun to wonder aloud about his ability to pull things together. So with his employees long gone, Bryce's was hard at work trying to get things back on track, pulling an all-nighter, something he had done regularly since returning to work. Bryce was an aficionado of the real estate development business and his work ethic was second to none. It was what he had always relied on since he decided to take over his father's company straight out of college. Most of the execs at the company thought the young upstart was too naïve to run the daily operations of the multi-million dollar company, but he quickly proved his worthiness of the title. He cherished these late night work sessions; aside from the occasional sound of a vacuum from the cleaning crew, the silence was golden. Marcus had offered to come back to the building to give him a hand tonight, but true to form Bryce turned him down.

Minutes turned to hours as Bryce worked with sniper

like focus. He was so engaged that the sound of the phone ringing startled him. With office hours long over he was shocked to hear his office line ringing at that time of night and assumed that it could be a wrong number. His first thought was to not answer it but his curiosity got the best of him.

"Hello," he said as he picked up the phone and put it to his ear. "Hello," he said a second time after receiving no answer just before the line went dead.

He quickly hung up the phone but before he could get back to work it immediately began to ring again.

"Hello…." he said once again but still no answer. "Hello!" he said this time his frustration was evident in his voice. Just as he went to hang up he heard a sinister laugh begin on the other end of the phone. "Who is this, Marcus?" he asked thinking it was his right hand man. But the voice on the other end of the phone just continued to laugh. Bryce hung up the phone and chalked it up to some juveniles playing a prank. Slightly thrown out of his zone but not enough to stop working, he quickly shifted his attention back to his task, only to be interrupted again when the lights in his office went black.

Bryce stood up from his desk and slowly felt his way through the oversized office to the door and out into the hallway, which except for the exit lights over the stairway, was pitch black too. He waited for his eyes to adjust to the darkness, then made his way towards the elevator, knowing in his mind that it wouldn't work but still willing to try he pressed the button. Nothing, he thought to himself now knowing that he had to make the long trek down the stairs. His recently healed leg immediately started to ache with just the thought; Bryce slowly walked over to the door and entered the dark stairwell.

He was halfway through his descent when he thought he heard footsteps in the stairway a couple flights beneath him. He stopped for a moment to try and listen for the footsteps but there was none to be heard. He continued the journey a few more floors before he thought he heard the footsteps again. This time he looked over the railing and called out to see if someone was there, but if there was someone there they were cloaked in darkness and didn't respond. Bryce figured the noise he had been hearing was actually the echo from his own footsteps in the empty stairwell. All the events of the past months had started to make him paranoid. Just as he took a few more steps that haunting laugh from the earlier phone call began to echo throughout the stairwell and those footsteps returned.

"Who is that?" he asked. "Who's there?" he shouted as he began to race down the flights of steps two at a time. The faster he moved the further away the sound became until he heard the door leading to the parking garage open and slam shut. Bryce made it to the bottom of the steps just a few seconds later, reached for the door and swung it open, only to be blinded by a bright light being shined directly into his face.

"Oh, I'm so sorry Mr. Edwards," said Teddy, the rotund night security guard with the cornrows in need of maintenance, as he lowered his flashlight. "I didn't know you were still in the building sir."

"It's ok Teddy," an out of breath Bryce replied. "Did you see who just came through this door?" Bryce asked desperately hoping he had caught a glance of the mystery person. But it was to no avail as Teddy explained that he had just come from the breaker room and Bryce was the only person he had seen in the building in hours. With the darkness hiding the disappointment on his face, he stepped out into the parking garage and tried to survey the structure for the person responsible.

"Everything alright Mr. Edwards?" Teddy asked.

"Yeah, just fine," Bryce answered just as the click signaling that the backup generator had kicked in sounded. "Have a good night." he said while making his way over to his car which set alone on that level of the parking garage.

Approaching the driver's side Bryce could vaguely see something sitting on the passenger seat of his car, but could not quite make out what it was in the limited light. He opened the door of his car to get a better look, the interior light of the car made it clear that it was a ball and jacks, used to play the popular kids game jacks. "What the fuck…is this somebody's idea of a joke?" he uttered before slamming his door and starting his car.

CHAPTER ELEVEN

It had been more than a few months since Bryce had enjoyed some of the night life Atlanta had to offer and Diamonds of Atlanta seemed like the perfect place to make his return. Dressed in a Pyrex Vision hoodie, black jeans and a pair of Jordan 6's he seemed to be trying to be low key. But the Gold Cuban link chain, table full of Ciroc bottles and the dozen of strippers dancing naked in the sea of hundreds in front of his table served as a PSA— Bryce was back and single. And just like usual Marcus wasn't far away, standing to the left of his friend with a stack of money in his hand, whispering into the ear of the super thick waitress, with the long black weave and blond swoop in the front. Just like his cohort, Bryce was on the prowl and his status afforded him options that many of the club patrons didn't have. He could hand pick whoever he wanted to spend the evening with. And by the way his eyes were locked on the light skinned beauty with tattoos covering her arms and back, he had made his choice. It was obvious by the way she stared at him like they were the only two people in the club, as she seductively moved her bare body to the music that she had chosen as well. Bryce tossed a stack of hundreds in the air and watched as it rained down over her, once again he felt like the king of the city and tonight she would get to see his crown jewels.

With his best friend engaged in a flirting session with the sexy dancer, Marcus scanned the room looking for someone to take home with him. But as he surveyed the club something else caught his attention.

"A bruh, ain't that ol' boy right there? The nigga from the party with Mia?" he said tapping his friend.

"I don't know is it?" Bryce asked.

"Yeah that's him right there with Rodney, Kim's husband." Marcus declared.

"With Rodney?" Bryce chuckled. "Mia and Kim got them out here on a play date, he must be all the way in now," he said continuing to laugh.

"Yeah I feel you," Marcus said as he joined in on the joke. "But you good with that?"

"Good with what?" Bryce retorted. "Him and Mia? I ain't stressing that shit bruh. You see where we at?" he said looking around at the naked women for emphasis. "I ain't worried about nothing. Matter of fact I'm gonna send them a bottle, show em it's no hard feelings."

Christion and Rodney stood by one of the stages tossing money at a few half naked women, when Rodney noticed the waitress carrying the bucket with a bottle and sparklers shooting from it heading towards them. It was a normal occurrence to see that in a strip club but it wasn't until she stopped in front of them that it caught Christion's attention.

"Yo what's this? We didn't order this," he said to the beautiful server.

"I know, it's from him up there," she said pointing to the VIP section of the club where the two businessmen sat.

"Oh that's Bryce," Rodney said as he turned seeing the familiar face.

"Nah, I'm good you can send that back. We alright over here." Christion informed her refusing the gesture.

"No, hold up, you can leave that right here, thank you." Rodney interjected.

"Yo I don't want that shit, fuck he think he is? I can buy my own bottles. He ain't the only one with money." Christion said voicing his anger.

"Let me explain something to you, sending that bottle back isn't a good look. It makes it look like you feel he's a threat, when at the end of the day you took his girl, so you winning, feel me?" Rodney schooled Christion. "So we gonna pop this bottle, get drunk on him and continue enjoying ourselves, 'cause I don't get to get out the house like this a lot," said the family man.

"Yeah I feel you." Christion said laughing at the married veteran.

∗ ∗ ∗

Bryce sat on the side of the bed in the plush master bedroom of his swanky Buckhead condo. The 1.1 million dollars he paid to live at the top of building on Peachtree was certainly worth every penny. He hopped up off the bed and walked over to the window and pulled the drapes back allowing the daylight to welcome him to a new day. The bright light shining in the room made the exotic beauty with the tattoos sleeping in his bed pull the covers over her head to avoid having to wake up. With the window in the room going from floor to ceiling, that was a battle she quickly lost and Bryce knew what he was doing. He had done it so many times before. Last night was fun but last night was over. He was ready for her to leave and like someone who had also done this dance before, she quickly got out the bed and began to get herself together.

"Where do you keep your towels?" she asked as she strutted naked towards the bathroom.

"In the closet on the left," he said admiring her sexy nude body, he continued to stare until she disappeared into the bathroom. Hearing the water from the shower turn on,

Bryce was tempted to join her for a little more playtime but decided against it, maybe not now but she had the type of pussy he definitely planned on revisiting.

Bryce's phone started to ring. He thought it was the car service he had prearranged to pick the female up and take her home, but that thought disappeared once he seen a number he recognized.

"Mr. Edwards, you have to hurry up and get here. Your house is on fire," was all he had heard before hanging up, he couldn't even remember who it was that had made the call. "You gonna have to cut that shower short, I gotta go," he screamed into the bathroom.

"Urrgh," replied the beauty from the shower clearly unhappy with being rushed. Bryce could care less as he picked up her shoes from the foot of the bed and stalked towards the bathroom to speed up the process.

With his mind moving as fast as his Porsche, Bryce raced towards his home. Turning onto his block he was greeted by the flashing lights and the sound of sirens from the fire trucks trying to save the massive estate from succumbing to the blaze. Bryce spotted members of the housekeeping and kitchen staff standing on the side of the road and jumped out his car to make sure everyone was okay and that they all had made it out safely. After finding out everyone was accounted for he began to question them about what exactly happened but nobody seemed to know anything. Bryce stood helpless watching fire fighters battle the violent fire for hours. He had been through his share of tragedy and although this paled in comparison, he couldn't help but think to himself, this shit can't be happening. What else can go wrong?

CHAPTER TWELVE

The scent of scorched wood resonated in Bryce's nostrils, invoking memories of the tragic plane crash that claimed his family, as he canvassed the area where parts of his house once sat, with the fire investigator and two detectives. The once immaculate estate hadn't been completely destroyed and it had sustained enough damage that the entire structure needed to be rebuilt. Losing his house was one thing. He had enough money to build a bigger and better home, but replacing the pictures, family keepsakes, and memories he lost in the blaze would be virtually impossible. He didn't have a lot of things to remind him of his childhood and family, but all he had, had been in that house.

Navigating through the ruins Bryce used his foot to push aside some debris revealing a partially burnt picture in a frame. He kneeled down, picked up the picture to get a better look. Wiping the soot off the picture revealed an image of him and Tremaine that once hung in his office. It was one of his most cherished possessions; one of the few pictures he had of his childhood friend and the fact that it survived made him smile just a bit and he began looking around to see what else could be saved. Searching through the remains seemed all too familiar, here he was once again needing to pull the charred pieces of his life from the ashes and put them back together.

"Mr. Edwards could you come over here for a second please?" the fire investigator shouted from across the rubble.

"You see this?" he asked as Bryce joined the group. "Exactly what I suspected, this wasn't an accident this was arson." The man said pointing to the bright red gas can.

"Arson?" Bryce asked.

"Yes Mr. Edwards," said the middle aged white detective with the salt and pepper hair.   "Arson. Do you have any idea who would want to burn down your home? Any enemies?"

Bryce paused before answering, not sure if he wanted to let the two detectives in on what had been going on as of late. "No… no enemies that I know of," he answered.

"You sure?" said the young black detective. "People don't just go around burning other people's houses down for no reason. I'm sure a man of your stature has made his share of enemies."

"Like I said not that I'm aware of," Bryce responded not liking the cops' tone.

"What kind of insurance you got on a place like this? I'm sure you stand to collect a nice amount of change from this fire," the detective continued to poke.

"Are you serious man?" Bryce asked clearly pissed off at what he was insinuating.

"We just have to explore all options in cases like these," said the white detective. "You'd be surprised what people will do to get themselves out of a jam. But if you're saying it's not you and you don't have any enemies, I would suggest you start looking a little closer to home.

"Closer to home?" Bryce inquired.

"Yeah, maybe there is someone around you who's not as happy with all your success as you think."

"I don't think so," Bryce declared.

"Most people don't, but it's something to think about. Here's my card. If you think of anything give me a call," the detective advised Bryce before walking away with his partner.

The two men made it back to their car before the younger detective said anything to his partner.

"So what you think Hirsch? You think he's hiding something?"

"I don't know Jones, but clearly you do." Detective

Hirsch said.

"Something just doesn't sit right with me about him. Didn't he get ran off the road a few months back?" Jones asked.

"Yeah, and?"

"And now his house gets torched. These rich motherfuckers always have skeletons in their closets; it's just a matter of time before they start falling out."

* * *

Mia floated through the hallways on her way back to her office. The day she had worked so hard for had finally arrived. She had just been offered to become a partner at the firm. She tried to remain as calm as possible, but the joy in her face was a dead giveaway once Angela laid eyes on her. Angela knew Mia almost better than Mia knew herself; she had worked for her for the last 6 years and could always tell when something was up with her. The day had been dragging along so far and Angela wasn't about to pass up an opportunity to get the scoop on what was going on with her boss.

"Spill it." Angela demanded.

"Spill what?" Mia asked.

"It's all over your face, something is up and from the look on your face it's good." Angela said. Angela was secretly hoping it had something to do with Mia and Christion. She was the only person in the office who knew that the two of them were an item. It was an open secret between the three of them. Angela would hold Mia's calls in the middle of the day, so that her and Christion could get in midday quickies in her office. Mia would say she was bouncing ideas off him about some of her cases, but Angela knew better.

"Ok, Ok, don't say anything to anyone but I just got offered to become partner," Mia said in a whisper as if someone was listening.

"Congratulations," Angela exclaimed, truly happy for the woman who had become like a mentor to her. "That is really great, I'm so happy for you."

"Nothing is final yet, but they are just waiting on an answer," Mia revealed. "Can you do me a favor and have Christion come to my office."

"Ok," Angela replied. "Is there anything else you need?"

"Lunch. Order something, anything, my treat. I'm starving."

Mia stared out of the window in her office with her dreams of becoming partner at her finger tips, all she had to do was say yes. But what once seemed to be a no brainer now didn't feel that way. For some strange reason she was having second thoughts. She was deep in her thought when Christion stuck his head into the door and flashed that smile that sent tingles through Mia's panties.

"What's up partner?" he said breaking her

concentration..

"How do you know..."

"Good news travels fast, you know nothing gets past me." he said as he walked in the office and sat down in front of her desk. "So how you wanna celebrate?" he asked indicating he was down for one of their midday meetings.

"Shut up nasty," Mia said blushing. "I haven't given them an answer yet."

"What you waiting for?"

"I don't know...just want to give it some more thought."

"Huh? This is all you've talked about and now you got cold feet. I'll never understand you Mia."

"I know. I just want to make sure. You can never be too careful."

"I guess you're right."

* * *

"Arson? Yo bruh, that's crazy," Marcus said into the phone, shocked by the news.

"I know. I need to find out who is behind this shit before someone gets hurt. This shit is getting out of hand." Bryce said.

"Hell yeah, somebody got it out for you bruh. You definitely need to get to the bottom of this shit. Somebody making attempts on your life and shit." Marcus said sounding concerned.

"Yeah I know, what you doing tho? I had wanted to get up wit you and talk about this shit, try to figure something out," Bryce explained.

"I ain't doing nothing, I'll be your way in a few. I got to take care of something real quick then I'm there," Marcus proclaimed.

"Take care of what?" Bryce asked.

"Nothing worth talking about."

"Aight, see you in a few." Bryce said before hanging up.

Marcus stood at the foot of the bed stroking his penis as he watched her rubbing her clit while on all fours.

"Damn your ass is fat," he said as his manhood began to swell in his hand.

"I know," she said as she licked her finger and slowly stuck it in her asshole knowing it would drive him crazy.

Marcus couldn't take it anymore; he had to taste her. He climbed on the bed behind her and stuck his face in her plump ass and began eating her pussy. Her sweet taste made his dick reach its maximum potential as her juices began to squirt out uncontrollably.

"Put it in," she begged in between soft moans, which instantly became louder once she felt his girth as he entered her from behind. The sound of their flesh slapping together could barely be heard as she moaned with every powerful stroke. The faster he stroked, the louder she became until she was ready to explode. "Oh my God!" she yelled out.

"Right there, right there, Oooh I'm cumming, I'm cumming on this big dick."

Marcus didn't break his rhythm as she collapsed on to her stomach; he continued to fuck her as hard as he could. He knew she liked it rough and he enjoyed giving it to her. "Oh your pussy is so fucking good," he said between strokes.

"Don't cum yet Marcus, I want you to put it in my ass," she said causing him to stop pumping, just hearing her say those words almost made him cum. He pulled out of her juice box and slowly inserted himself in her ass. At first he pumped slowly until she got comfortable with his size in her ass. She moaned out in pleasure as he picked up the pace, fucking her even better than before. She could feel herself about to cum again and asked for him to go harder and faster. Marcus felt himself reaching his peak as well, making him pump faster and faster until he climaxed. "Oh shit, LaTrice I'm cumming," he said before collapsing onto her back.

Latrice laid there trying to catch her breath. Although she really couldn't stand the way Marcus was she couldn't deny the fact that nobody fucked her like he did. It was the reason why unknowingly to any of their friends they had never stopped. After laying there for a few more moments her attention turned back to the conversation Marcus just had with his friend.

"What was all that about with Bryce?" she inquired.

"Nothing," Marcus said trying to downplay his talk with his friend.

"Do I look stupid to you? Answer that right," she warned before he could say something sarcastic. "What you mean somebody making attempts on his life? Somebody trying to kill Bryce?"

"I don't know it's just been a lot of weird shit going on lately: him getting ran off the road, the shit at his party, now somebody burned his house down," he informed her.

"Burned his house...hold up, what! Does Mia know about all this?"

"I don't talk to Mia like that. The shit in the newspaper, she can read," Marcus said sounding annoyed.

Latrice's cellphone started vibrating on her nightstand. When she peeked to see who it was, she saw Kim's name flashing across the screen. She had already decided not to answer it due to the fact that Marcus was there but did after he informed her that he was about to leave and got up and went into the bathroom. She picked up the phone but didn't answer it until she saw him close the bathroom door.

Marcus turned on the water and began running the shower in the bathroom. He walked over to the linen closet and retrieved a towel and washcloth. He was just about to get in the shower when he decided to listen in on what the two females were discussing. He eased up close to the bathroom door and pressed his ear up against it trying to get a better listen. He stood there listening to their entire conversation, letting the shower run while pretending to be in it.

CHAPTER THIRTEEN

Bryce removed his hard hat and placed it on the waiting hook, after finishing a tour of the structure that would eventually be The Phoenix; he was pleased with the progress. After shaking a few more hands and speaking with the foreman in charge one last time, he was ready to leave. But not before buying everyone lunch to show his appreciation for their hard work.

Bryce navigated his way through the streets of midtown Atlanta, trying to figure out where he wanted to stop for lunch. He had a craving for Mexican food and decided to head straight for Uncle Julio's but upon turning onto Peachtree Street he ran into traffic that was backed up and barely moving. Lunchtime traffic was usually a little thick, but this was different, it wasn't until he saw the emergency vehicles zooming passed that he realized it had been an accident up ahead causing the logjam. After about 15 minutes traffic began to move again but at a snail's pace. His stomach was now growling and he was growing impatient. Bryce's once cool demeanor had begun to disappear as of late. He had become easily agitated and short tempered, clearly because of the effects of his world being turned upside down and someone making attempts on his life. Now stopped in traffic only a few feet from Uncle Julio's, something -or better yet, someone -grabbed his attention. Sitting at a table on the patio outside the restaurant, engaged in what looked to be a very interesting discussion was Erica, but that wasn't what had him taken aback. It was who she was having lunch with that had a look of shock across his face.

"That's Marcus? What the fuck is he doing with her?" Bryce said to himself out loud as though someone was in the car with him,after witnessing his best friend sitting so close and looking rather cozy with the closest thing he had to a girlfriend at the time. Bryce didn't want to jump to conclusions but it didn't look right to him. His first thought was to pull into the parking lot and walk in the restaurant and see their reaction, but his name had been in the paper so much lately he couldn't afford any more negative press. He instead turned into the Wendy's parking lot directly across from them and parked so that he had a clear view of them without them being able to see him.

Bryce watched as the two talked, ate, and ordered rounds of drinks. He was so upset that he had long forgotten about how hungry he had been. Bryce had decided he had seen enough. Unable to watch any longer he started his car up and pulled out of the parking lot heading to his apartment. Thoughts were racing through his mind and he felt himself getting angrier by the moment,and he took a couple of deep breaths and tried calming down.

"Nah I'm bugging Marcus is my brother, he wouldn't do that," he began to tell himself.   "You know what I'm just gonna call this nigga and see what's up," he said snatching his phone off the passenger seat. After a few rings Marcus answered. "Yo what's up?" Bryce asked calmly.

"Ah what up bruh?" Marcus answered.

"Ain't shit, what you up to?" Bryce questioned.

"Nothing 'bout to walk into this muthafuckin' gym, get my workout on," Marcus said.

"Yeah, I feel that," Bryce said trying to remain calm now that his best friend had just lied to him. "You not going into the office today?" Bryce asked.

"Nah I told you I was taking a couple days off. I got some running around to do." Marcus responded him.

"I don't remember you saying nothing about that." Bryce proclaimed.

"You buggin, I told you a few days ago." Marcus tried

reminding him.

"Nah nigga, you buggin', you never told me that. But it's whatever, I'ma talk to you later." Bryce said before hanging up the phone.

He instantly thought back to what one of the detectives had said to him that day at the aftermath of the house fire about looking at the people close to him. Bryce knew he had no real enemies, but maybe blinded by jealous rage Marcus had become one. He had always played second fiddle to the popular millionaire and maybe he was tired of it. Why else would he be doing these things? Why else would he be pursuing Erica? He wanted what Bryce had and was willing to do anything to have it. No matter what the reason, he was convinced Marcus could no longer be trusted. Erica on the other hand was on her way out anyway he told himself. She was just a space saver, local news chick surviving more on her good looks than her brain. He never saw her as a viable option to begin with. She was fun but definitely not wife material.

The elevator doors opened up and Bryce stepped off into the massive living room of his luxury penthouse. Being betrayed by his best friend was weighing heavy on him as he made a beeline straight to his bar. After dropping a few ice cubes in a glass he poured himself a glass of Ciroc and went and stood by the large window in the living room. He stood there sipping his drink and enjoying the view, letting everything soak in. He had worked so hard achieving all his success but here he stood at the top of the world alone— no family, no friends and no Mia.

Bryce stared at the empty glass in his hand as he swirled the remaining ice cubes around when he heard the phone indicating someone was on the elevator trying to come up to visit. He walked over and picked it up.

"Who is it?" he asked.

"It's me, let me up."

Bryce recognized the voice it was Erica, he paused before answering her.   "What you want?" he asked sarcastically.

"What do you mean what I want? Stop being silly and let me up." Erica said.

"I don't feel like company right now," he said.

"Bryce what is wrong with you? Let me up," she said ignoring him.

"What part didn't you understand?"

"Why are you acting like this?" she asked sounding confused.

"I don't know, Erica. How about you go visit Marcus and offer him some comfort, cause he gonna need it. Cause I ain't fucking wit' that nigga no more and I ain't fucking wit you either. So get the fuck off my elevator and get the fuck out my building."

"No Bryce, it's not like that. Let me explain…" she said

before hearing the line go dead.

Bryce walked across the room back to his bar and refilled his glass. He picked his phone up off the bar and dialed Marcus's number.

"Bruh, what's up?" Marcus said as he answered the phone.

"That's what I'm trying to figure out." Bryce said.

"What you mean?"

"You still at the gym? I'm 'bout to come through." Bryce inquired.

"Nah I left already."

"Already?"

"Yeah I got in there and changed my mind." Marcus explained.

"You a fuckin lying ass nigga. You never was at the gym. You were at the Mexican joint with shawty. I saw you, you a foul ass nigga."

"Nah bruh, you got it fucked up, it ain't even like that," Marcus intervened. "Trust me it's not what you think."

"Trust you? How I can trust a fuck nigga? You jealous nigga, you want what I got? You could have come at me like a real nigga instead of doing all this sucka shit."

"You think I'm behind all this shit? You drunk or something? We brothers I don't get down like that, I would never." Marcus expressed.

"Fuck you, I ain't got no brothers and you can clean out

your office your services are no longer needed."

"Bruh you trippin', you paranoid, it ain't what you think. I'm..."

"I don't give a fuck what it is, you dead to me." Bryce said before hanging up his phone and throwing it across the room as if it were their friendship.

CHAPTER FOURTEEN

The loud sound of the vacuum cleaner was being drowned out by Jill Scott's beautiful voice blasting from the entertainment system in Kim's living room. It was the soundtrack she used to keep her motivated while cleaning her home. The daily duties of being a housewife could get boring and overwhelming at times. With all the cooking, cleaning, and tending to the needs of her family, a little Jill playing in the background always seemed to make things run a little smoother. Kim had already cleaned the entire upstairs of the Craftsmen style home, taken out her dinner to thaw, fed RJ and put him to sleep for his nap. She was now going to clean her husband's man cave in the basement, all while keeping an eye on the time as she waited for her daughter's bus to arrive dropping her off from school.

Kim grabbed the baby monitor and headed downstairs, to what she knew would be her biggest cleaning job in the house. Rodney, her husband, did most of his entertaining in their basement: hosting fight parties and the weekly gathering of friends for the Falcons game. Reaching the bottom of the stairs her worse fears were confirmed; the fellas had left a disaster site— the remains of a Monday Night Football game.

Kim was hard at work getting the basement back to respectability, when she thought she heard her door bell ringing upstairs. Kim raced up the stairs into the living room to lower the volume of the music then walked to the front door to see who was ringing the bell.

"Who is it?" she shouted through the door, but received no response. She looked through the peephole and didn't see anyone either. After asking who was there a couple more times, she walked back in the living room and increased the volume on her music back to where she had it. She darted up the steps to peek in on a still sleeping RJ before heading back to the basement to finish cleaning.

Returning to the basement Kim could feel a draft in the room that she hadn't felt before going upstairs. She immediately went to check the windows to make sure they were closed. After seeing they were all shut tight and still feeling the wind, she walked across the room to the double glass doors that led out to the backyard. The closer she got, the more she could feel the cold. Now standing in front of the doors, she could see one of them slightly ajar. As she approached the door to close it, she felt herself being pulled back and a gloved hand go over her mouth and a knife being pressed to her neck. She tried to let out a scream, but the gloved hand clenched her jaw, shutting her mouth. Kim fought to release herself to no avail, she was being overpowered by the assailant who was in her home. Still she was unwilling to concede defeat. Although at that moment she feared for her life, all she was able to think about was her baby asleep upstairs and how she would willingly give up her life to save his.

"You scream and you die," were the instructions the masked man uttered before removing his hand from her mouth, pressing the point of the knife deeper into his victim's neck. Tears streamed down Kim's face. She had no clue what he wanted or why he was there. Her fears only heightened when she turned, seeing his piercing dark eyes staring back at her through his mask. Before she could ask either of those questions he began to strike her in the face over and over again until she became dazed. He dragged her by her hair over to the couch and began to rip at her black tights. Kim tried to sit up and put up as much of a fight as she could but still dizzy, she couldn't do much. He placed his massive hand around her neck, choking her while using the knife to rip at her clothes. Kim looked up at the ceiling and said a silent prayer. She asked God to allow her to make it through this horrific ordeal alive and to let it be over before her daughter got off the bus. Not fully aware of her intruder's intentions, she would have rather died first before her daughter was there to witness or be victim to the terror she was enduring inside of her own home.

It felt like a ton of bricks hit her stomach when he rammed his penis inside her, tearing the outer layer of skin on her vagina as he entered. She moaned in agony with every thrust. The harder he fucked her the tighter his grip grew around her neck until she was almost breathless. He noticed her passing out and quickly released her neck.

"Oh no bitch, you gon' stay up for this," he grunted, grabbing the half empty vodka bottle off the end table and turning her over, before jamming it in her ass. Pain shot through her body like an electric current. Kim screamed in agony as he ripped at her rectum until it bled profusely. Kim almost wished he would just kill her, rather than to deal with the pain. She closed her eyes, trying to drift out of her body.

"You die when I say you die, bitch," he growled removing the bottle from her ass and striking her with the butt of it opening up a gash on her forehead. He then twisted the cap off the vodka and poured it into the open wound. The burn made Kim cry out in pain. He tossed the empty bottle across the room smashing it up against the bar and continued beating her with his fist until his arm became tired. The heartless intruder stood and grabbed Kim by the hair, dragging her lifeless body off the couch and up the stairs; far from done, he hadn't quenched his thirst for blood yet.

Lyric got off the bus in front of her house. She immediately noticed that her mom was missing. It was rather unusual for her mom not to be there to meet her when she arrived from school. Most times she was standing on the side walk when the bus pulled up or standing in the door waving at the bus driver, but she was always there. Her absence made the young girl a little nervous but she walked up the steps leading to her house expecting her mother to swing open the door at any time, holding her little brother in her arms flashing that smile that made her smile. Once she made it to the top of the steps she could hear the loud music blasting from behind the door. Hearing Jill Scott calmed her nerves some. She knew that meant her mom was cleaning the house from top to bottom. Lyric thought to herself that her mom must have gotten so wrapped up cleaning, that she lost track of time and probably didn't even realize her bus had come already. Lyric rang the bell hoping her mother would hear it over the loud music, but after a few minutes of ringing the bell constantly with no answer, the nervous feeling she had getting off the bus returned. She didn't want to be stuck outside until her mom realized what time it was. Thinking fast she decided to try going around the back of the house and seeing if she could get her mother's attention. But as she got around the back of the house she saw that one of the doors to the basement was open.

She was a couple feet into the house before noticing all the blood splatter everywhere: on the carpet by the bar was a broken liquor bottle, on the couch was a pool of blood with a trail that led upstairs. Tears filled the wells of Lyric's eyes and began running down her face as she screamed out for her mother. The sound of the young girl screaming could be heard echoing through the entire neighborhood. Lyric's heart was racing as she cried uncontrollably walking up the steps into the kitchen. The smell of burnt flesh greeted her nostrils as soon as she opened the door. The kitchen had been ransacked and looked like a scene out of a horror movie. There was bloody hand prints on the lower part of the wall, like someone had been crawling trying to get away. Lyric followed the hand prints into the foyer, when she seen something no child should ever have to witness, the bloody and battered body of her mother laying naked in her own blood. Lyric screamed at the top of her lungs shocked at the mere sight.

$$* * *$$

Mia had raced to the hospital as soon as she got the call from a hysterical Latrice. She had called Christion to tell him to meet her but could barely contain her emotions and had to hang up before telling him what was going on. She had cried the whole way there, the news that her best friend was clinging to life after being brutally raped and beaten and the fact that her 8 year old god-daughter was the one who found her mother was almost too much to bear. She had to take her medication during the ride just to stop a panic attack from coming on.

Walking into the lobby of the hospital with tears streaming down her face, Mia spotted Christion waiting for her and instantly fell into his arms, collapsing under the enormity of the situation. Christion's embrace was exactly what she needed at that moment, as he held her and guided her to the elevator. Stepping off the elevator and joining Rodney and Latrice in the waiting room, you could feel the anxiety as they all awaited word on Kim's condition. Rodney was speaking with the police officers, while trying to relay information to Kim's mother, who was flying in from New Orleans. Mia sat holding hands with Latrice praying for their friend and for Lyric who had found her mother's lifeless body. Mia thought back to seeing Bryce wake up in the middle of the night from the recurrent nightmare of losing his parents and best friend, so she knew how losing a parent could affect a person for their entire life. She didn't want Lyric haunted by those same memories. After waiting for what felt like an eternity the room fell silent as the doctor entered and walked towards them.

* * *

Marcus sat in the pitch black room unable to move. He was tied to the chair with his arms handcuffed behind his back. His head was still spinning and he could hear ringing in his ear, the results from just coming to after being struck in the head with a foreign object— that was also the reason for the large gash on his head that was bleeding profusely. He couldn't see anyone, but he could feel he wasn't alone in the room.

"Who's there?" he asked trying to get all his faculties together. His eyes were burning with the mixture of blood and sweat pouring into them and made it hard for him to focus. "I know you hear me!" he shouted. "Say something muthafucka, you gonna hide in the shadows. What type of nigga do that?' he asked again.

Before he could say another word he had heard the striking of a match. He shifted his eyes around the room until he located the little flicker of light. He watched as the light got bigger and brighter and he began to smell cigar smoke. He could hear the person get out of the chair and walk towards him. Still unable to see, Marcus started to cough with the thick cloud of smoke that was blown in his face. The dark mysterious figure calmly walked over cracking the blinds to let the slightest bit of light in, just enough for Marcus to see the face of his captor.

"Who are you?" Marcus asked, receiving no reply but seeing the gun the man was holding for the first time.

His heart began to pound in his chest even harder than before seeing the man lift the gun and point it towards him. He was in close quarters with a psychopath wielding a gun. Marcus now knew he was in deeper than he could have ever imagined. "Who are you?" he asked again still not getting an answer out of the man.

"You not gonna answer me? Answer me muthafucka!" Marcus shouted now realizing he probably wasn't going to make it out this situation alive. "Let me up out this chair." Marcus continued his rant. "If I get out this chair, I'm gonna take that gun and shove it in ya ass." He said wiggling around in the chair trying to free himself.

Marcus's antics only drew a smirk from his captor, who watched over him like prey, but still offered no response. The man's silence was killing Marcus and his fear began to show.

"Why are you doing this?" Marcus finally broke down and asked after becoming frustrated trying to escape his restraints. The question seemed to resonate with the gun wielding menace. His smirk suddenly disappeared and was replaced by a look of pure evil. Marcus knew he had hit a nerve. "Tell me, Tell me muthafucka, why...why are you doing all of this?"

"Because I can." The man boldly stated before squeezing the trigger putting two in Marcus's chest and one in his forehead.

CHAPTER FIFTEEN

Bryce pressed down with all his weight trying to help Tremaine close his over packed suitcase. The day had come for them to return to Atlanta and by the look on Tremaine's face he wasn't in a rush to get back. He had gotten a long glimpse of the life he had longed for and to him it was ending too fast. He had taken his time packing and hadn't done a good job of it, but he didn't care because the longer it took them to close his suitcase, the further they were from leaving.

"Dang, you had this much trouble closing this bag before?" Bryce asked out of frustration.

"I didn't have that much stuff before." Tremaine reminded him, referring to all the shopping they had done with his parents since being on the island.

Tremaine finally got the suitcase closed and all the feelings of not wanting to leave became a reality— it was time to go.

"What's up Tre, why you looking like that?" Bryce asked finally noticing the look on his best friend's face.

"Just thinking about going back to the home, that's all. Being here with your parents all week just made me wish I had this all the time. You got it made, you get to travel all over the place, you have two parents that love you, you never have to worry about money. I mean yall are rich. This is the life, who wouldn't want all of this." Tremaine expressed.

"I know it may seem that way but money isn't everything. Money doesn't stop all the white kids I go to private school with from calling me nigga every day. I hate going to that school. I wish I could go to a regular school with regular kids, but I can't. I can't even have fun like a normal kid. I can't go ride my bike outside because my parents are so scared someone will kidnap me trying to get money out of my dad. That's why they buy me so much stuff, trying to keep me happy or busy. But half the time its stuff I don't even want. That's no way to live Tre, I'm not welcomed in the neighborhood I live in and I'm not safe in my dad's old neighborhood. I don't fit in anywhere. You think I got it made? Think again." Bryce informed his friend.

"Still look good from where I'm standing." Tremaine countered.

"You boys ready?" Mr. Edwards asked, sticking his head in the room door.   "C'mon your mother is waiting downstairs. You know she hates being late."

Tremaine grabbed his suitcase off the bed and looked around at the massive bedroom and the beautiful view one last time before following Bryce out the room...

* * *

Bryce sat staring at the picture of the two childhood friends that he pulled from the remains of the fire. The image captured how close the two were and looking at it always gave him mixed emotions. Their friendship was one of the last things he remembered being regular in his life. Neither one of them wanted anything from each other except friendship. Bryce had questioned everybody's intention since, something he hated having to do but knew it was necessary for someone of his stature. Tremaine would have never imagined being rich and powerful was this hard.

His deep thought was interrupted by the buzzer signaling someone was on the elevator looking to come up. Bryce stood from the couch, walked over and picked up the phone.

"Who is it?" he asked.

"Detectives Hirsch and Jones, Mr. Edwards. Can you let us up? We need to speak to you." Detective Hirsch spoke into the phone.

The elevator doors opened up and the two detectives stepped off into the luxury penthouse. They were both impressed but didn't show it.

"What do I owe the pleasure of this visit, gentlemen?"

Bryce asked. "I haven't thought of anything new regarding the fire or who could be responsible for it." Bryce informed them, choosing to not reveal his suspicions about Marcus.

"We are not here about that." Detective Hirsch answered. "When was the last time you spoke to or saw Marcus Gilyard, Mr. Edwards?" he continued.

Bryce was caught off guard by the line of questioning. He wondered if they knew he too thought Marcus was the culprit. "I haven't seen or spoken to him in a couple of days, maybe a week."

"Really?" Detective Jones said in amazement. "Aren't you guys best friends? I know I don't go that long without speaking to my best friend. How 'bout you Robert?" he said looking at his partner. "Have you guys had a falling out as of late?"

"Where is this going? What does Marcus have to do with yall being here?" Bryce asked.

"Well Bryce, I'm sorry to have to tell you this, but we found Marcus's body early this morning." Detective Hirsch informed him.

"What?" Bryce said in shock feeling like he was just kicked in the stomach. "How? What? Where?" he stumbled trying to find the words.

"His car was found abandoned and he was in the trunk of the car. He was shot 3 times and it looked like he had been there for a couple of days."

"Do you know who did it?" Bryce inquired immediately forgetting what the two had recently gone through.

"No not yet, but we have some ideas." Detective Jones assured him, seeming to imply Bryce as a possible suspect.

"I done had enough of you. You got something you wanna say to me man?" Bryce asked turning his attention towards Jones, fed up with his insinuations and sarcasm. After just learning his friend was dead and feeling guilty of accusing him of being responsible for all the chaos in his life, Bryce was in no mood to deal with his attitude. He had let his comments the day of the fire slide but wasn't willing to afford him the same luxury at the moment.

"What the fuck is your problem? You got something against me?" he asked the detective.

"Yeah, I don't like you and I don't trust you. You run around this city like some type of hero but I know it's more to you— I can feel it. You're hiding something and I'm gonna figure it out and when I do I'm gonna use it to crush you, you privileged muthafucka." Detective Jones confessed.

"Are yall done?" Bryce said.

"Yeah that will be all. Like I said Bryce if there's anything you think of that could help us, give me a call." Detective Hirsch said sticking out his card in his hand.

"I got one already." Bryce countered refusing the card. "Now if yall don't mind I have a funeral to plan so I can bury my best friend."

* * *

Mia sat in silence next to Kim's hospital bed with tears running down her face. The beeping sound of the machine keeping her friend alive was the only sound in the room. The sight of Kim laying there lifeless with tubes everywhere broke Mia's heart into little pieces. All she could think about was who could be responsible for putting her friend in that hospital bed. Who would do such a thing to a person that sweet and kind hearted. Her and Kim had been friends for years and never had so much as an argument. Kim was always the voice of reason for Mia, the level head she relied on when things would spin out of control. She had been there for every break up with Bryce and was there to lend support when they made up. Kim was always there for Mia and now it was her turn to return the favor.

"I promise you, I will be here every day until you open your eyes." Mia whispered to her friend while rubbing her hand. "You take as long as you need. I know you could use the rest." She said trying to make light of the situation as she forced a smile in between tears. But inside she knew that her friend was lucky to be alive and she wasn't quiet out of the woods yet. The doctors said because of the swelling on her brain there could be a chance of brain damage.

"Hey baby," Christion said as he softly knocked on the door and stepped inside the room. He could see the pain in

Mia's face as she sat next to her battered friend. Seeing Kim laying there clinging to life really hit home for him. He felt for her husband Rodney; he could only imagine how he felt, thinking to himself how he would if it had been Mia laying in that bed. Christion walked over and stood next to the bed staring down at Kim. He was speechless looking at all her burns, cuts and bruises. After a few seconds he finally found his words.

"Whoever did this is a monster," he said shaking his head. "To do something like this to another human being is truly reprehensible." Christion placed his hand on Mia's back and began rubbing it. He knew she needed his support. He wanted nothing more than to be there for her.

"You ever think we're on the wrong side?" Mia asked.

"What do you mean?" Christion responded.

"As lawyers we defend these criminals; people who are responsible for things like this. You don't ever think about maybe we are on the wrong side."

"After something like this I can see why you would feel like that, but every defendant isn't guilty. I try to focus on that. Keeping the innocent free."

"Yeah, I guess." Mia hadn't said anything but she was now reconsidering accepting the partnership at the firm.

CHAPTER SIXTEEN

"I don't want to do this anymore. This is not what I signed up for." Erica announced as she frantically paced back and forth inside the motel room. The realization of being in way over her head was weighing heavy on her and she was now reconsidering her involvement. "I was just supposed to get some dirt on Bryce that we could use to blackmail him. You never said anything about killing anybody." the reporter said. "You lied to me Omar."

Omar sat shirtless on the bed, camouflaged by a cloud of weed smoke, uninterested in Erica's newly found fear and trepidation. A hardened criminal, he saw Marcus's death as collateral damage— a means to an end. Marcus was on to him. During his meeting with Erica at Uncle Julio's he had asked her to use her investigative skills to help him uncover who he was. Erica reported back to him about what Marcus was up to and Omar made the decision to eliminate him, something he secretly took great satisfaction in doing.

"I didn't lie to you. That was never the plan, but what was I supposed to do? Let him ruin all our hard work?" he stated giving her a menacing stare. He was fully committed to his plan and he wasn't about to let anybody get in the way of seeing it through. Omar watched as she continued to pace. She was on the verge of cracking and he knew he needed to do something to calm her down. "Come here," he ordered her. "Smoke some of this, it will calm your nerves."

Erica walked over to him and grabbed the weed and took a long pull, thinking to herself how did she ever let him talk her into this. But in her heart she knew how, she was in love with Omar. She had always been and she was willing to do anything for him. Erica West was originally from Ohio. That's where she first encountered Omar while attending college, at an off campus party. He was out in Ohio hustling and after dating for only a few weeks she allowed him to move into her apartment and set up shop. She quickly fell for him and the lifestyle he provided— the classic good girl bad guy relationship, the danger and excitement turned her on. He took good care of her all through college, even after he left Ohio and returned home. So when he wrote her from jail explaining how he had a million dollar lick she was all in— no questions asked. She wanted to see him on top again.

After a few minutes had passed and her high kicked in, Erica's nervousness had subsided and her sexual arousal intensified. Omar's strength and confident swagger made her body temperature rise as he sat up leaning against the headboard of the bed, the bulge in his jeans on clear display. Erica crawled across the bed like a sexy kitten and began licking on his chiseled six pack while unbuckling his pants, reaching her hand inside and pulling out his semi erect penis. Erica slowly swirled her tongue around the rim of his dick, stroking the shaft with her hand bringing him to a full erection, before taking all of him in her mouth until she felt him in the back of her throat causing her to gag up spit which she used for more lubrication. Erica rubbed on his balls as she quickened her pace. Omar enjoyed the view as she made his dick disappear and reappear again over and over. Erica was extremely wet, the anticipation of feeling him inside of her was driving her crazy. She slid her panties to the side, straddled him and started riding him reverse cowgirl style. Omar gripped her ass as she went up and down on his dick, her pussy becoming wetter as she began to cream. Omar felt himself on the verge of exploding and started to pump harder and faster until he erupted inside of her.

While the two laid there in a sexual bliss, Omar rolled over and ran his fingers through her hair. "You trust me?" he asked.

"Yes." she answered still in a euphoric state.

"Have I ever let you down?" he asked.

"No never," she responded.

"So I don't want you to worry. I'm gonna make everything right. Now get up and get in the shower so we can get out of here," he said smacking her on the ass.

Erica rolled off the bed, grabbed her clothes and headed towards the bathroom. Before entering she looked back at him and smiled, knowing in her heart that he would make things better. She truly believed in him and trusted in his plan. More than anything she couldn't wait to get her hands on some of the money he had promised her.

Omar smiled back at her, fully aware that she had no idea of the more sinister motive behind all his scheming. She thought she was his queen in this game of chess he was playing, but to him she was just another pawn and a pawn's only purpose was completely suicidal.

∗ ∗ ∗

Bryce exited off I-85 onto Pleasant Hill Road. It had only been a few days since Marcus's funeral and finding out who was responsible for his death had become Bryce's number one priority. He knew that if he could find out who killed Marcus most likely he could find out who had been terrorizing him. That's why he didn't hesitate to meet with Erica once she texted him saying she had information regarding Marcus's death. She expressed remorse for meeting with him behind Bryce's back and knowing how close they were she wanted to share her findings with him first before going on TV to report them.

Pulling up into the remote motel, Bryce was full of nerves. He hoped he was about to find out who the responsible party was and wanted nothing more than to put this all behind him. Bryce parked his car in front of room 116 and hopped out. His eyes scanned back and forth, checking his surroundings, trying to make sure he hadn't been followed or wasn't being set up. Walking up to the room Bryce could hear the TV from inside through the door. Knowing that Erica wouldn't be able to hear him at her door Bryce decided to knock hard, but when his fist hit the door it pushed open slowly. Bryce could see directly through the room and there was no sign of Erica. He could see the bathroom door cracked and steam coming out of it. He stepped into the room calling out Erica's name, hoping she could hear him from the shower, but she didn't respond. Bryce walked over to the TV, which was blasting slow jams from the music channel and turned it down before calling her name again. Nothing changed still no reply. Bryce decided he would peek in on her and call her name letting her know he was in the room. He walked over to the bathroom and stuck his head in the door, but before he could call out her name, he saw Erica laid out on the floor. Bryce swung open the door and raced over to her, upon approaching her he could see blood pouring out of a large hole in her temple from an apparent gunshot wound. Bryce also noticed the gun laying to her side, still partial in her grasp and quickly realized that she had taken her own life. Erica's eyes were still wide open so Bryce squatted down next to her to close them. He placed his hands over her eyes and shut them. Something else caught Bryce's attention, the gun she was holding looked familiar to him, it was his gun; the one that had been stolen from his office by the intruder during his birthday party. Bryce's face filled with confusion but before he could find some sort of clarity he felt the cold steel of a gun press up against the back of his head.

"Don't move motherfucker." the voice said. "You're under arrest!"

Bryce turned his head slightly and could see two uniformed police officers now in the bathroom with him, weapons drawn. With his attention preoccupied after finding the beautiful woman's body, Bryce hadn't even heard the gang of police that had converged on the room. He rose to his feet with his hands locked behind his head before the officer grabbed him and slapped the cuffs on.

CHAPTER SEVENTEEN

"The body you see being removed from the hotel room is that of Erica West, reporter for the Channel 2 news. Police received a tip about a disturbance at Motel 6 in room 116 and when they arrived on the scene they say they found Bryce Edwards—yes, multi-million dollar real estate developer Bryce Edwards, standing over her body. Police haven't said if this is a suicide or a homicide investigation. But we do know Mr. Edwards has been taken into custody for questioning. More details to come on the 10 o'clock edition."

Mia stared at the TV in shock. She had known Bryce more than half her life. She knew in her heart that he couldn't be responsible for the crime he was suspected of. Mia's phone rang as soon as the news went to commercial.

It was Latrice asking her if she had seen what the news was reporting. After discussing their feelings about Bryce's predicament the two women hung up. Mia hit the button on the remote and paused the TV. She screamed across her apartment for Christion, who had just gotten out the shower.

Christion walked into the living room wearing a pair of grey sweatpants and a white wife beater. "What's wrong Babe? Why you screaming like that?" he inquired.

"Look," was all Mia said pointing the remote at the TV and pressing play.

* * *

Bryce sat quietly in the squeaky chair inside of interrogation room 2, with his fingers interlocked on the table in front of him staring at the one way mirror. He felt like he was being watched and his hunch was corrected. On the other side of the mirror stood Detectives Hirsch and Jones observing his every move and analyzing each one.

"So what do you think?" Hirsch asked his partner, then took a sip from his cup of coffee.

"I told you it was just a matter of time," Jones replied. "I knew it was more than meets the eyes with this fucking asshole. I knew he was hiding something."

"Well let's go see what it is." Hirsch declared.

Bryce saw the door opening up and the two detectives stepped in. Hirsch sat in the chair directly across from him and Jones grabbed a chair from the corner of the room and sat it right next to Bryce, facing him purposely getting as close as possible to Bryce; trying to make him uncomfortable. Knowing the detective's ill feelings for him, Bryce was ready for any tactic Jones decided to throw his way.

"So Mr. Edwards, people seem to have a tough time staying alive around you." Jones said. "First your so called best friend and now a woman that you've been seen with around town on many of occasions, ends up dead and you're found standing over her body. How do you explain all these coincidences?"

"As just that, coincidences." Bryce answered.

"And you expect us to believe that?" the detective retorted.

"It's not about what you believe, it's about what you can prove. And I know I've done nothing wrong so there's nothing to prove." Bryce responded.

"You'd be surprised what I can prove with a little effort." Jones informed him showing his intent to do whatever he could to see Bryce behind bars.

"What my partner is trying to say is, if you're not telling us the truth we will find out." Detective Hirsch intervened. "Now can you explain how you ended up in that room with Ms. West's body in that remote location?" the veteran detective asked, already having read Bryce's statement he had provided to the officer's at the scene but needing to hear it from him.

"Like I told the other officers, I got a text from Erica saying she had information regarding Marcus's death and she wanted to meet. When I showed up I found her dead in the bathroom." Bryce stated. "I showed the other officers the text."

"That doesn't prove anything" Jones said jumping back in even more animated. "I think you're hiding something. You wanna know what I think reading this text?" Jones said reaching in his pocket and slamming Bryce's phone on the table. "Got some info U might be interested in. B4 I go public." He said reading the text aloud. "I think Erica found out you killed Marcus and was threatening to expose you unless you met with her and agreed to pay her, but you decided it was better to kill her instead."

"You have a great imagination." Bryce said. "It's only one problem asshole, Erica committed suicide. I found her with the gun in her hand." Bryce said raising his voice slightly.

"I've been on this job a long time and I know a staged crime scene when I see it and that scene was definitely staged." Detective Hirsch proclaimed.

"Well like I told your partner, prove it." Bryce replied in frustration.

"Ok," Jones said rising to his feet. "You arrogant son of a bitch. How 'bout this for proof?" he said pulling out a plastic bag with the gun from the scene. A gun that belonged to Bryce. "See we know this gun is registered in your name and I'm willing to bet that when we run forensics it will match the gun used to kill Marcus as well. Now what do you have to say?" Jones said with a smirk on his face knowing that he had his man.

"He doesn't have anything to say." Mia said as the door of the room swung open. "And you two should know better than questioning my client without his lawyer present. Now if you're not going to charge Mr. Edwards with a crime, this little interview is over." Mia declared.

"Hold on Ms?" Jones started.

"Armstrong."

"Ok, Ms. Armstrong, we have more than enough evidence to hold your client. We have him standing over a dead body and a murder weapon believed to have been used in another homicide," insisted the overzealous detective.

"You have nothing, you have a stolen gun found in the hand of a woman who committed suicide, clearly distraught over killing Marcus Gilyard. Now if you'll excuse us." Mia said motioning for Bryce to follow her as she walked out the room.

The ex-lovers walked through the precinct without saying anything to one another. Bryce was at a loss for words. Here was the woman who he believed hated his guts coming to his rescue. He was on the verge of losing everything. In his mind it would be just a matter of time before Detective Jones found a way to make his perception of things a reality, true or not. Bryce badly needed someone to believe him and hoped Mia was that person. What she thought meant more to him than anything anyone else could say. He could deal with the media and other naysayers thinking he was guilty but if Mia believed he was capable of murder and that he was a monster it would crush him.

Upon exiting the building they were immediately met by a flood of reporters with microphones asking questions concerning his guilt; while cameramen and photographers captured images of his fall from grace. Bryce remained quiet, continuing to move down the steps. Mia did the same while repeating they would have a statement at a later time. Eventually a couple officers cleared the way for them to reach the bottom of the steps into a gated parking area.

Bryce turned to Mia as they reached the parking lot of the police station. "Mia I don't know what made you come here but I thank you for your help. I just want you to know that I did not kill Erica or Marcus." Bryce firmly stated.

"I know that Bryce," Mia acknowledged. "You may be a lot of things," she sarcastically continued. "But a killer isn't one of them."

Bryce lowered his head and shook it from side to side. It all seemed like a bad dream that he could not wake up from. Someone had run him off the road, crashed his birthday party, burned his house down, murdered his best friend and was now framing him for murdering Erica. And to top it all off of he had a renegade detective hell bent on seeing him held responsible for it all.

"Bryce what is going on?" Mia asked. "Why is all this happening?"

"I don't know," he said still refusing to tell her all that had been going on.

"Tell me the truth Bryce, for once. You are always keeping things hidden, that's not gonna help you this time." Mia insisted.

"I am," he said unconvincingly.

"Well I suggest you find yourself the best lawyer money can buy, because those detectives in there are not going to stop until they get their man and in their minds that's you." Mia informed him as if he didn't know.

"I thought I had a lawyer?" a confused Bryce asked. "What was all that back there?"

"My civic duty." Mia sharply stated.

"Really?" Bryce asked in disbelief. "Mia I know you have no reason in the world to want to help me right now, but I need you. I don't know why any of this is happening truthfully. Maybe it's karma for the way I handled us, but I ain't no killer. And I can't go to jail for something I didn't do." Bryce pleaded his case like he was already on the stand as tears filled his eyes.

"Take the case Mia," a voice from behind him said. Bryce turned to see who was there and saw Christion standing by his car. He had given Mia a ride down to the station and was actually the one who suggested she should go help Bryce, after he asked her feelings about his guilt after watching the story on the news. Mia had voiced her strong belief in Bryce's innocence, stating that she knew him better than anyone and to her surprise Christion told her she should go help her ex, reminding Mia that their responsibility to keep the innocent free superseded her and Bryce's rocky relationship.

"Bryce, you've met my boyfriend Christion." Mia said.

"What's up?" Christion said sticking out his hand showing he held no grudge from some of their earlier encounters.

Bryce still not sure of what to make of him, but not wanting to upset Mia stuck his hand out to meet Christion's. "What's up," he said.

Mia was so attracted to Christion at that moment. She admired the way he was handling the entire situation and thought to herself how she was going to fuck the shit out of him when they got home. After pausing to give Bryce's request more thought she finally turned to him. "Yes I will take the case."

CHAPTER EIGHTEEN

News trucks, cameras and reporters lined the street in front of the building that housed Edwards Developments. Bryce spotted them as soon as he turned the corner. Lucky for him they hadn't noticed the black SUV with dark tints he was driving pass right in front of them and pull into the underground garage. He knew they would be on the lookout for one of his many exotic rides and decided to go with the nondescript vehicle trying to avoid having to answer any questions. The horde of reporters camping out every day had become bad for business and being accused of murder had resulted in some investors retracting funds on various projects including his grandest— The Phoenix.

Edwards Development had become a sinking ship that was taking on water fast with people jumping ship left and right. Bryce knew he needed to plug some leaks. So he scheduled an early morning meeting with the board of directors of the company to discuss strategy on how to deal with the recoil of him being associated with Erica's death.

Bryce could feel the tension in the air walking through the office. The once vibrant place had become lifeless, filled with employees who at one time couldn't wait to see him; now uncomfortable to make eye contact. Yolanda wasn't one of those people. She refused to believe the mud being slung on her boss's name. She hadn't even asked him about the accusations, not once; her only concern was his mental well-being, constantly reminding him that she was praying for him. She also had become his eyes and ears inside the office even more so than before. She would overhear executives at the company plotting and would inform him of their intentions and today was no different. As she saw Bryce approaching her she sprang from her seat and waved to him to hurry up and follow her into his office. Bryce unaware of what was going on followed her with a confused look on his face.

"Bryce something is up," she whispered as if the room had been bugged.

"Huh?" an even more confused Bryce asked.

"Every member of the board has been here for over an hour locked in the conference room." Yolanda informed.

"Really?" Bryce asked in shock, "the meeting wasn't supposed to be until 9."

"Exactly, something is up and they told me to have you come to the meeting as soon as you arrived. Something isn't right."

"Hmm," Bryce said as he thought to himself for a second. "Yeah something is definitely off. Thanks for the heads up Yolie." Bryce gathered his thoughts and composed himself before heading to the conference room.

Bryce's abrupt entry surprised almost everyone assembled in the room causing immediate silence. But the look on the board members' faces spoke volumes. Yolanda was right, something was definitely up and Bryce was ready to find out just what it was. Walking to the seat left vacant at the head of the table, he sat signaling the end of the secret meeting and the beginning of the one he had called.

The young CEO had brought his father's company to heights no one could have imagined in a very short time, but was seeing it all collapse even faster. He wasn't going to sit idle, allowing the media and the police to tear his well-constructed empire down. More importantly was the fact that his family name was being dragged through the dirt and he was to blame. Mia would handle a court case should charges eventually be filed, but she couldn't help him in the court of public opinion and that was what was hurting the bottom line at EDI. He thought he had some ideas to fix things but before he could explain them, the board member sitting right next to him interrupted him.

"Bryce I know you are wondering what we all were doing here before you came," the older black man with salt and pepper hair said. "And I don't want to drag this out any longer than it has to. We took a vote and we prefer that you would step down as CEO. Your flashy lifestyle and bad choices have always been a reason of concern for some of the members at this table, me included. I personally thought you should have never been named CEO, but out of respect for your father's wishes I didn't object. But your mistakes are starting to affect all of us, and you have not only embarrassed this company, you have shamed the legacy of your great father."

Bryce sat quiet for a moment allowing what the man had just said soak in, his eyes canvasing the room, trying to see if he had any allies left. To his surprise he found none. He had made these men more money than they could ever spend and this was how they showed their thanks, by attempting to a coup. Bryce tried to find a way to calm the fire that was building in his belly, but was unsuccessful.

"Step down?" he asked rhetorically. "I built this company into what it is today. My last name is on the front of this building. Not to mention I have stood behind some of you in this very room, during some of the toughest times in your lives, never wavering in my support." Bryce said rising to his feet. "You know who are." he said looking at several individuals at the table.   "I've done a lot for a lot of people in this room and now yall are ready to turn ya backs on me and throw me out on my ass? Where's the loyalty?"

"It's not about loyalty," one of the other older gentlemen at the table chimed in. "And this is not personal. This is about business and frankly Bryce you're bad for business."

"Not personal? I can't tell." Bryce retorted staring at the board member who had been sitting next to him. "I know a lot of you hated the fact it was in the will for me to be in charge of this company. I know some of you thought I was too young when I took over and I busted my ass every day to prove I was worthy of the position. The first chance yall get to snatch this company from under me yall try it. That's how you honor my father's dying wish?"

"Let's just take a step back everybody," said the board member seated at the far end of the table, who looked to be the oldest man in the room. "I personally don't believe the allegations against this young man. I knew his father for a long time, longer than anybody in this room, and I know if he has an ounce of his father in him, nothing the news is saying is true. Now I could be wrong but I'm willing to bet I'm not."

"How can you be so sure?" the man with the salt and pepper hair spoke up again.

"Just a gut feeling." the elder said. "I propose that we hold off on voting until we see how everything plays out."

"I think we should be proactive and handle this now."

"And what make you CEO?" the elderly man joked. "We all know Bryce is the best at his job. I'm just saying let's not rush to judge."

Bryce watched as the temperature in the room began to change. The looks on their faces said they were at least warming up to the thought of letting him remain in place. He was finally feeling like something was going in his favor for the first time in a long time, but before he could claim victory he had to hear the official decision.

"All in favor say I," the elder said, as Bryce watched as hands raised and he heard I's fill the room slowly. "Ok, but there is one more thing Bryce," the man said. "You gonna have to remain low key for a while and step back from the day to day operations just to give this time to play out or blow over. For business purposes, it's not good for investors to have to see you right now."

Bryce nodded in agreement signaling the end of the meeting, but not everyone was as happy as Bryce.

* * *

Mia sat at her desk, scanning through a stack of papers she had been going over for the last few days. Unbeknownst to anyone, Mia had launched her own investigation into the things that had been going on with Bryce, going back to him being ran off the road. She had more than a few connections down at the police station and was able to get her hands on the accident report, as well as, the report from the fire at Bryce's home. Although Bryce hadn't been officially brought up on charges yet, she was trying to get ahead of the ball. They had history and even though she was no longer with him, she didn't want to see anything happen to him. She was the best at what she did and she planned on getting to the bottom of all of it. She had a lot on her plate. She was still hoping to aid police in finding who was responsible for the attack on Kim as well. Mia truly wouldn't sleep well again until that person was placed under the jail.

"What's up babe?" Christion asked, peeking his head into her office startling her, breaking her concentration. She hadn't even told him that she had begun her own investigation into Bryce's incidents. Although he had given his blessing, Mia was doing more than she was leading on and not wanting to give the impression it was anything more than just trying to help. So she decided to keep it to herself.

"What you working on?" he asked.

"Oh, nothing important," she lied. "Just looking over some papers I had never got to," she said closing the folder. "Why what's up babe, you need some time?" she said flirting, knowing how he loved having sex in her office, all while slipping the folder of documents into her desk and out of sight.

"No, I'm about to get out of here. I'm done for the day, just came to say bye. I'm gonna go play some ball."

"We still on for dinner tonight right?" Mia asked as she rose for her desk and walked towards him.

"Of course," he said flashing that smile that drove her crazy. "What you bout to do?" he inquired. "You still going to the hospital?"

"Yes, I actually need to be getting out of here now too."

"Ok I love you," he said before kissing her on the cheek and exiting her office.

CHAPTER NINETEEN

Latrice looked up from her seat next to Kim's hospital bed upon hearing the door open and saw Mia walk in. The two friends, along with her husband, alternated sitting with Kim, talking and reading to her. Kim had begun to show significant signs of improvement. Although doctors had upgraded her condition they decided to keep her in a coma until some of the swelling went down on her brain. After her survival being in question, Kim was now expected to make a full recovery.

Latrice stood to hug Mia, far from the glamorous seductress that was her normal look. She was dressed in a black hooded sweat shirt and jeans. Her eyes were red like she had been crying and she looked as though she was in desperate need of some rest. The last few weeks had been hard on her. She was mourning the loss of Marcus like everybody else, but she was taking it a little harder than anybody knew because of their secret ongoing sexual relationship. With the stress of Kim almost being killed, on top of running her business a good night's sleep was hard to come by. So when she seen Mia, she was happy, hoping that she could get home and get some sleep.

The two chatted for a few before Latrice headed out and Mia took a seat next to Kim and began telling her about her day, like she did every time she came to visit. Mia had seen Christion do the exact same thing on a few occasions when she accompanied him to visit his grandmother in the very same hospital. Until recently she couldn't understand how he could sit for hours and have a one way conversation with someone in a coma, but she realized when you care for someone the way she did for Kim it wasn't hard at all.

Time seemed to fly and before Mia knew it Rodney was walking in the hospital room along with Kim's mother. Mia stood and hugged both of them. After updating Rodney on what the doctor had to say during his rounds, she said her goodbyes and headed for the elevators.

While waiting for the elevator Mia's thoughts went back to Christion and his grandmother. Since she was in the same hospital, Mia decided she would stop by her room a few floors up and look in on her. She felt it was the least she could do, after all Christion loved his grandmother more than anything. He would always entertain Mia with funny stories from his childhood spent with her and all the things he had learned from her. He would always say, "I wouldn't be the man I am if it wasn't for her." He told Mia how he wished the two could have met and how his grandmother would really love her.

Mia could not remember the room number, only the direction they had walked once getting off the elevator. She hoped she would recognize it when she saw it. Walking slowly down the hallway with her eyes bouncing from right to left, Mia realized the room had been on her right side after she passed the water fountain, but she still couldn't remember if it was the first or second room after the water fountain.

Mia stuck her head into the first room and smiled once she realized she had found the right room after seeing the elderly woman with all silver hair lying unconscious in the bed. Though she looked so peaceful in that bed, Mia knew the cancer spreading all through her body and into her brain was slowly killing her. Mia was startled by the sound of the toilet flushing in the bathroom, unaware that anyone was in the room. When the bathroom door opened a brown skinned male who looked to be in his mid-30s emerged. The unknown man seemed to be just as surprised to see Mia in the room as she was to see him. The two stared at each other in confusion, neither saying a word for what seemed to be a minute but was more like ten seconds. The silence was broken by the unknown man.

"Umm may I help you?" he asked.

Mia looked back at the woman lying in the bed again, this time getting a better look and said. "Oh I'm sorry, I'm in the wrong room. I was looking for Mrs. Annette Washington's room."

* * *

Bryce threw his keys on top of the breakfast bar, happy to be home. His day had started with dodging reporters, then the board members asking him to step down and to make matters worse he had gained a tail. While riding home he noticed the unmarked car with the two detectives working Erica and Marcus case following him. Whoever was behind this had succeeded in turning his life upside down and into a living hell. Bryce was slowly going crazy and it had become harder and harder to hold it all together. He grabbed his cell phone and scrolled down and pressed Marcus's number in the phone. It rung once before Bryce realized what he had just done and hung up. He was so used to calling his best friend when he was stressed, he did it without thinking. Bryce could not understand why everything was happening to him but he really needed someone to talk to.

He thought of calling Mia. He really missed being able to talk to her the way they used to. They would lie in the bed for hours and just talk.It was something they could always do, ever since high school. They would spend hours on the phone discussing their problems, what college they wanted to go to and how successful they hoped to be. They always spoke about spending their lives together and enjoying each other's success. Now here they were exactly where they hoped to be, but far away from where they thought they'd be at the same time. Bryce knew for him and Mia to ever get back to the place they once was he would finally have to come clean with her about the secrets he had been keeping.

He scrolled through his call log and decided to take a chance on calling Mia. After seeing her with Christion he wondered if she still held a place for him in her heart. After all it did take him to convince her to help him. Truth was that he could afford any lawyer in America, but he wanted Mia representing him. He saw it as a way that he could at least be around her, even if it was only temporary. He was banking on the fact that not only was she good and she hated to lose, but that they had history and no matter how bad of terms they were currently on, she would never want to see him in jail.

Bryce could feel his heart in his throat as he listened to the phone ring on the other end; he was ready to hang up when she answered.

"Hello," she answered.

"Hey Mia, this is Bryce, you got a minute?" he inquired.

"Yeah, what's going on?"

"I really need to talk to you, it's important," he stressed.

"Something about the case?" she wondered.

"Yes and no," he stated.

"Bryce, if you can't separate yourself from our past in order to.."

"Mia they are trying to take my father's company from me," he blurted out interrupting her in mid-sentence.

"What?"

"Yeah they are trying to vote me out because of all this shit. This shit is weighing heavy on me. I just needed someone to talk to." Bryce confessed.

Mia paused taking in what she had just been told. She knew Bryce better than anyone and could hear in his voice he was really stressing. "Ok, I'm just leaving the hospital now. I'll be over to you in a few."

"Alright," Bryce said before hanging up the phone. He was thankful she decided to meet with him. He thought to himself how amazing of a woman Mia was and how good she had been to him. He knew he had messed up with the way he had handled their relationship and he probably didn't deserve her. He recognized she was happy with Christion and was reluctantly willing to let her go. But he felt he owed it to her to tell her the truth about breaking off their engagement. Not only for her to have a better understanding but for him as well, he was ready to get it off his chest.

CHAPTER TWENTY

Bryce showed Mia into the living room of the luxurious apartment. Seeing how this was her first time there, he offered to give her a tour but she gracefully declined. She knew Bryce had good taste and she liked the new place from what she could see from the living room, but she had no interest in a tour. She was used to his extravagant living quarters. She had visited some of the most beautiful places on earth with him and stayed at some of the most expensive places. Besides she wasn't there for all that, she was already questioning herself about deciding to show up.

Bryce asked if she would like a drink. When she requested a Pepsi, it caught him off guard because he was thinking more in terms of an alcoholic beverage. As he disappeared into the kitchen Mia begin looking around the room, thinking to herself how many women must have been through his apartment in the past few months. Her nostrils flared and her lips curled up as she shook her head just as Bryce re-entered the room, holding a glass full of ice and a Pepsi. Noticing her face Bryce asked if everything was alright, breaking her train of thought.

"Yes," she quickly answered. "So what is it that you wanted to talk about?"

"Everything," he replied. "Should I lay on the couch?" he said playfully as if Mia was a therapist. When Mia didn't crack a smile he realized he should just get to it. He could always make her smile and laugh but that was no longer the case. Staring into the face of the woman he was supposed to spend the rest of his life with and her not feeling anything was a pain his heart wasn't ready for. He felt like he had been kicked in the chest. How could he have been so stupid to allow this woman out of his life and push her into the arms of a another man. It wasn't about who was right or wrong for him at that moment, he just wished he could do it all over again. After all he had been through, looking at Mia sitting in his living room, he would marry her a thousand times. He wanted to grab her by the hand and take her upstairs and make love to her like it was his last night on earth. But instead he handed her the glass and soda and took a seat on the chair across from her.

"Like I was sayin' on the phone, I'm already stressed out

with this case hanging over my head. Now they are tryna snatch Edwards Development Inc from me. I've put everything into building that company into what it is, but now they are tryna throw me out on my ass."

"Can they do that?" Mia asked truly concerned. She had witnessed all his hard work first hand and knew how important his work at the company was, not only to him but to the legacy of his family.

"If I don't voluntarily resign, they could vote me out." He informed her. The look of fear in his eyes was one that Mia had only seen when he would awaken from his recurring nightmare. "They are treating me like I'm guilty."

"Well are you?" Mia asked honestly. Bryce glared at her as if to say really you too. "I just figured I'd ask," she said.

"What do you think?" Bryce questioned.

"It doesn't matter what I think."

"It does," Bryce insisted. "It matters, it matters to me," he said as his voice tailed off. "You probably know me better than anybody. You think I'm capable of doing what they're saying?"

"People change," Mia coldly replied.

Bryce sat back in the chair and folded his arms. "Yeah, I guess they do," he said referring to Mia's attitude towards him. He was starting to feel like placing the call to her was a bad idea. She was supposed to be there to help, but she wasn't. She seemed to be only making things worse. How could he have her representing him if she still hated him? Mia was the one having troubles separating her feelings from her job. "Is that my lawyer talking or my ex?"

Mia, clearly incensed by his question, rose to her feet knocking over her soda. "You know what fuck you! I don't have to be here. You need my help not the other way around," she stated unsympathetic to his issues. "I'm happy with my life. Can you say the same? Look at you, Bryce fuckin' Edwards, God's gift to the world. The man who has it all—please," she said sucking her teeth. "You're a miserable little boy with a bunch of toys and no one to play with. You can put on a front for the world but not for me. I've slept with you for years. I've seen you wake up in cold sweats; I've seen that look on your face before. You're still just a scared little boy on a plane."

"You think you know everything, huh? You got it all figured out," Bryce said getting up from his seat. "Do you know what it feels like to feel guilty to be alive?" he asked causing Mia to stop in her tracks of her exit march. "To be the one that always lives while everybody around you dies. Do you know what it feels like to lose everyone you got close to? Everyone I have ever cared about dies," he said with tears flowing from his eyes, years of penned up emotion filling every tear drop.

Mia wanted honesty, but she truly wasn't prepared to hear what she had. She had never given thought to the possibility of Bryce feeling guilty for surviving. For the first time in a long time she was at a loss for words. In front of her stood a man she once loved more than anything in the world and he was suffering. Bryce was a tortured soul with a broken spirit. Mia walked towards him, still unable to speak. Filled with so many emotions; she placed her hands on his face and began wiping away the tears. After a few moments Bryce placed his hands on top of hers, unexpectedly giving Mia chills. She wanted to pull her hands away but didn't. Bryce stared in her eyes; he could see the flood of emotions in her face. He slowly began kissing on her hand, then pulled her into him. Mia stared at his lips. She always thought they were so sexy and was her favorite feature of his. She couldn't help but want to lick them and stopped herself, but Bryce didn't— he leaned in and kissed her. Mia resisted at first, even attempting to pull away, only to have him pull her closer. Eventually she lost her inhibition and opened her mouth allowing his tongue to slip in.

With Mia's arms now wrapped around his neck, Bryce cupped her plump ass scooping her up off her feet. Mia wrapped her legs around Bryce, crossing her feet to secure herself, as he made his way over to the steps. As they reached the steps Mia began licking and sucking on Bryce's neck causing his dick to become rock hard.

Finally reaching the top of the steps, Bryce carried Mia towards the bedroomand pushed open the door, walking over to the bed before placing Mia gently on to it. Mia kicked off her boots and began removing her sweater as Bryce removed her pants and panties. With her clothes now off Bryce wasted no time diving face first into her shaved pussy; quickly flicking his tongue in and out of her only stopping occasionally to bite her on her thighs. Mia loved every minute of it. It had been so long since she felt his lips on her and the feeling was exhilarating. Bryce continued sucking on her clit while using his two fingers to penetrate her. Mia arched her back as she rose up off the bed slightly and moaned out, "suck it harder." Bryce obliged. Mia spread her legs as far she could giving him full access to her juice box, grabbing the pillow and placing it over her face, screaming into it as she reached an orgasm. It was like he had the blueprint to her body, he knew it better than anyone and knew just how to please her.

"Put it in," she moaned with her body still trembling. Bryce rubbed his brick hard manhood against her clit a few times before sticking it into her throbbing pussy. Mia welcomed him into her gladly. Her once moist pussy was now dripping as he pounded her rapidly, causing her to scream with every pump. Her noise only seemed to turn Bryce on even more as he pounded away. He missed being inside of her. He loved making love to her; it was something he had wanted to do for months. Bryce felt himself ready to explode;Mia could feel it too. She wrapped her hand around him grabbing his butt and pulled him into her as they both began cumming at the same time. Bryce collapsed on the bed next to Mia. They laid there breathing heavy trying to catch their breath.

* * *

Looking into the rearview mirror, Mia saw a confused woman staring back at her. On the heels of what had just happened upstairs in Bryce's house, she could no longer pretend that she didn't still have strong feelings for him. She also had strong feelings for Christion. Mia always thought there was no way for a person to be in love with two people but she now found herself having to reconsider that way of thinking. As she pulled out of the parking garage, she felt bad that she didn't feel guilty about having sex with Bryce. That's why she gave him a little more before she left. But she didn't want to end her relationship with Christion either; she didn't know what to do. One thing she did know was that she couldn't wait to get home and into her bathtub. It had truly been a long day. Unbeknownst to her she had been being followed since she left the hospital earlier that day.

* * *

Omar watched from his car as Mia emerged from the parking garage and into traffic. She was so beautiful to him. He almost felt bad about having to hurt her, but she provided the perfect opportunity to finally finish off his devious plan.

All the chaos he had created had finally brought her back into Bryce's life. That's what he wanted all along. Convincing Erica it was about blackmail and money was what he needed to tell her so she would do what he wanted: get close to Bryce and collect as much information about his comings and goings as possible. He wanted to know what made him tick; he needed to know his routine. And Erica supplied all of that, but he never wanted money. He took pleasure in slowly destroying the glamorous lifestyle Bryce flaunted around. He felt Bryce believed that he was better than everybody, that somehow his money made him untouchable. Bryce thought he was a God amongst men. Omar despised everything that the millionaire playboy stood for and relished the chance to show him differently. The pain Bryce thought he felt was nothing compared to what Omar was preparing for him. He was going to kill the one person Bryce had left, Mia. He was going to make Bryce watch him cut her heart out. Then he was gonna frame him for it all. Omar couldn't help but laugh to himself as he followed Mia in traffic. Reaching the light he watched her drive into the parking ramp connected to her building. As the light turned green he rode past her building without stopping. He was going to kill her for sure, but today wasn't the day.

CHAPTER TWENTY-ONE

Mia searched frantically through her office, but no matter how hard she looked she couldn't seem to find what she was looking for. She opened and closed desk drawers, straightened up all the papers on her desk and scanned though them, still nothing.

"Angela, could you come in here please," she called out.

"Yes," Angela said walking into the office watching as her boss pace back and forth.

"Was anybody in my office today?" Mia asked.

"No why?" the assistant asked.

"I'm missing a folder, an important folder. I had it

yesterday and I put it in my desk and now it's missing."

"Nobody's been in here outside of maintenance and we've never had an issue with them before," Angela reminded her boss seeing her beginning to stress.

"Yeah, you're right. Maybe I took it home without realizing it. Either way I'll find it."

"Find what?" Christion said as he entered the office.

"Oh hey," Mia said cracking a smile as he entered the room. It was the first time she'd seen him since her and Bryce hooked up. He had called last night to say he wouldn't be coming over due to how tired he was from working out. Mia pretended to be sad but was actually happy. It gave her time to snap out of the trance Bryce had her in after their sexual encounter. "I'm looking for a folder I had with some background info on Erica West."

"Oh ok, you thinkin' it could help you with Bryce's case?" he asked.

"Yes, but I had something I wanted to talk to you about. Ang, can you excuse us," Mia said. Angela nodded her head and stepped out the office closing the door behind her.

"So what's up?" Christion asked, sounding very interested in what Mia had to say.   "Everything ok?"

"So I'm at the hospital yesterday seeing Kim…"

"How is she doing?" Christion interrupted.

"A lot better, but that's not what I wanted to speak to you about." Mia informed him. "I'm at the hospital and I decided to check in on your grandmother," she said using her fingers to indicate quotations. "And I spoke with a family member of yours, Ms. Washington's grandson to be exact. He had no idea who you were. In fact, he said he had never even heard of you before. What do you have to say for yourself?" Mia said glaring at him as if her looks could kill. She had been through all of Bryce's lies in the past but she wasn't about to go through that again.

"What?" Christion said seemly unaware of what Mia was talking about. "Someone was in my grandmother's room visiting her?" he asked completely ignoring her line of questioning.

"Yes, yesterday when I went..."

"And ya just telling me this?" he asked slightly elevating his voice. "Mia we don't have any family out here," he reminded her, as he pointed his finger to his head suggest she should be smarter than she was being. "My grandmother only had one child, my mother, who only had one child, me. So whoever you spoke with at the hospital was not part of my family."

Mia stood there in disbelief. She had been so used to Bryce hiding things she immediately assumed Christion was guilty of the same thing. She hadn't given him the benefit of the doubt. She hadn't even questioned what the unknown man at the hospital was telling her. She just took it at face value and ran with it. She felt bad, after all she was a lawyer she should have questioned the man more, maybe she could have found the cracks in his story.

"What did he look like?" Christion asked, but before she could answer he continued. "Never mind I have to call the hospital," he said before walking out of her office.

As Mia sat down in the comfortable leather chair behind her desk, her mind went right back to the missing folder she had been looking for. She looked through her desk once again, after another unsuccessful search, she thought long and hard about where it could be. Just then she thought to herself to search her email for the file that was sent.

Mia logged onto her computer and began scrolling through her emails. Still she couldn't find it; it seemed to have disappeared into thin air. Mia thought to herself maybe she deleted it accidently, scrolling through her trash files still netted no results. As Mia scrolled down the screen something caught her eye; an old email sent from Marcus Gilyard's account that she had never seen. The subject line said: *Open and Read Immediately!!!* The date of the email was only a few days before Marcus's body had been found, that fact only made Mia click on it, opening it.

As Mia began to read the email, she couldn't believe her eyes. She had to put her hand over her mouth to keep from screaming. She had just found what Marcus was working on, and what she now believed was the reason he had been killed. Mia stood up from her desk and raced over to the door and locked it, then quickly returned to her desk and hit print on the screen.

Nothing happened, Mia checked her printer. No ink, shit, she thought to herself. Not wanting to send the information to any other printer in the office. Mia decided to go home and print out everything and continue reading all the information Marcus had collected.

Christion returned to Mia's office after getting off the phone with the hospital, only to find her gone. He walked over to her desk to see if her things were absent as well, signaling she was done working for the day. Leaning over her desk to see if her bag was gone, Christion bumped her desk moving her mouse, causing the screen on her computer to light up. Naturally he started to read what was on the screen. He was only a few lines in when he realized what he was looking at. Just like Mia he couldn't believe his eyes either. Marcus had maybe solved his own case from the grave.

* * *

Mia made it home in no time. Her heart was racing with adrenaline as she exited the elevator on her floor. She couldn't get her keys into the door fast enough. She wasted no time once inside dropping her bag and heading straight for her computer.

Omar stopped his car across the street from Mia's

building. He knew she was inside alone, he had pulled up a few minutes after her. He put on his blinker and turned into the parking ramp next to her building. Mia had no idea she was in so much danger; downstairs from her home was a ruthless killer who was willing to do the unthinkable to see his plan through, and she was his next target.

Mia hovered over her printer unable to contain her patience. She started snatching the printed pages out one at a time as they were finishing. When it was all done she sat down next to her computer and began going through each page. The more she read the more she couldn't believe her eyes. What Marcus had stumbled upon was something she wasn't prepared for; something that stretched beyond the realm of her wildest imagination. Mia couldn't help but become emotional thinking that what she was reading was the cause of Marcus's death and he had sent it to her almost from the grave.

The wells of her eyes quickly filled and it wasn't long before she was raining tears onto the papers on her desk. Filled with a vast amount of emotions and her mind racing with thoughts, Mia's body temperature began to rise and her breath felt like it was stuck in her throat. She started sweating and before she knew it she was in the midst of an anxiety attack. She jumped up from her chair and went into the kitchen to get a glass of water and her meds.

Filling the glass halfway with water, Mia popped two

pills in her mouth and downed them with the water. She removed her shirt, which was now soaked with sweat and walked back into the living room, sitting on her chaise lounge trying to regain her brief lapse of sanity. As Mia waited for her meds to kick in she began to feel groggy and everything seemed to be going in slow motion as she tried to stand up. Mia tried making her way across the living room into her bedroom but wasn't able to. After a few steps she collapsed onto the floor.

Looking up at the ceiling the room seemed to be spinning. As Mia struggled to remain conscious she could hear someone messing with her front door. Mia heard the door finally open, but was unable to clearly see who was entering her home before she blacked out.

CHAPTER TWENTY-TWO

Omar walked back and forth in the middle of Mia's living room, reading all the papers she had printed out. He couldn't lie, Marcus had done a ton of research, most of it very accurate. If they had been discovered sooner he would have been exposed and his entire plan would have been derailed. That's why Marcus had to go. Besides the fact that during the time he had been watching Bryce, he grew a strong hatred for his best friend as well. Omar enjoyed killing him. His twisted mind found pleasure in all he had done, but nothing would provide him as much joy as the look on Bryce's face when he killed Mia in front of him.

Mia could see the shadowy figure in her home but she couldn't quite make out who it was. The drugs were slowly wearing off, but she was still floating in and out of consciousness. All she knew was her head was killing her, a result of hitting it when she collapsed on her living room floor. Her mouth felt like cotton and she could feel the tape covering it. Starting to come to a little more she realized she was unable to move, she had been tied to the chair she was in. Still unable to completely focus on the figure she seen walking back and forth in front of her she began making slight noises as the pills wore off and the pain set in.

Omar heard the faint noise coming from Mia as she was trying to awake from her slumber. He grabbed the chair from her computer desk and sat it right in front of her, removing the knife and the gun from the small of his back before sitting down. He pulled his chair up as close as possible to Mia, to where she could feel his breath on her skin. He moved the hair from out of her face and ran his fingers through her hair before kissing her on the forehead.

The room slowly started to come in focus for Mia. It seemed as though it all came back at once and she was finally able to lay eyes on her captor. Mia's eyes grew bigger when she saw the knife and gun he held in each hand. She began trying to scream, but the duct tape over her mouth wouldn't allow her to. Omar, seeing this, just smiled.

"You got something you wanna say?" He grabbed the

edge of the tape and ripped it off her mouth, causing Mia to scream out in agony and he just laughed.

As the pain of having tape removed so viciously subsided, she was finally able to speak.

"Christion what's going on? Why are you doing this?" Mia asked confused as to what was happening. What was the man she had been dating for months doing stand over her wielding a gun and knife?

"Don't play stupid bitch you know what this is about. I see you found the shit Marcus was working on, huh?" he said grabbing the stack of papers and throwing them at her.

Mia couldn't believe the transformation she was witnessing. Gone was the smooth talking heart throb Christion, replaced by a man with a look of pure evil in his eyes. "Ok, so who are you really, because I know your name is not really Christion Bradford. I've seen the pictures of the lawyers from the firm you claimed you worked for in New York and you're not him. I also know he's been missing for months. Did you kill him too?" she asked boldly.

Omar laughed at the feisty woman. What Mia lacked in stature she made up for in fearlessness. "Who I am is not important. You should be more concerned about what I am," he said as he pressed the point of his knife into Mia's throat.

"So you gonna just kill me now? I thought you loved me?" Mia asked pretending to be unfazed by the knife at her neck.

"Love?" he said chuckling before he smacked her hard across the face causing blood to leak from her mouth. "That shit ain't gonna work Mia. I have no emotional strings to pull. I'm not a bitch like Bryce," he taunted.

"Ok so I know why you killed Marcus. Why kill Erica?" she asked.

"So many questions, I should have left that tape on," he replied. Clearly not willing to play Mia's game, he was fully in control and was about to show her. He balled up his fist and struck her across the face again. The blow almost knocked Mia unconscious again. Omar picked up the remote and turned on the stereo and turned the volume up. He then took his knife and began causing cuts all over Mia's body; she screamed with every incision. After being satisfied with the amount of wounds he had inflicted Omar disappeared into the kitchen. Upon his return Mia noticed him carrying the bottle of bleach from underneath her sink.

Omar slowly poured the bleach over the wounds he had caused on Mia. She screamed like a wounded animal as the bleach touched her skin. He remained unfazed by her cries for him to stop, after a while she stopped begging and just screamed for someone to help her.

"Nobody is coming because nobody can hear you," he said taunting his victim. "You know what though, you take an ass whipping a lot better than Kim."

Mia couldn't believe what she was hearing. She had

been sleeping with the man responsible for raping and beating her friend almost to death. He was truly a monster. He had been in Kim's house, around her kids, hung out with her husband, he sat in the hospital and comforted Rodney the day she was found. How could someone be that evil? she thought to herself.

"Why?" she screamed through tears. "Why Kim? She never did anything to you muthafucka," Mia said through clenched teeth.

"She saw me having lunch with Erica," he stated. "Couldn't have her running around with that information now could I? The bitch just wouldn't die."

"Why rape her you evil bastard?" Mia asked still crying uncontrollably.

"Why not," he said nonchalantly.

Mia's heart felt as though it would give out at the thought of him doing the exact same things to her. She had once craved him but now cringed at the thought of him touching her. Confused as to what his motives were, she tried pulling it out of him using her superior lawyer skills. "So where did you learn how to pretend to be a lawyer so well?" she asked.

"A lot of days in the library at Clinton Correctional."

"What are you doing this for Christion? Or whoever you are. Why me? Why Bryce?"

"Oh Bryce knows why, he just needs to be reminded.

You, you were just a pawn in my game of chess. But now you're just bait. Watch Bryce come running," Omar put his gun to her head. "Now you gonna call em and tell em to meet you at that construction site at that high rise he buildin'."

Omar picked up her phone and dialed Bryce's number and put the phone to Mia's ear and his gun to her head.

Bryce picked up on the second ring seeing Mia's name flashing on his phone. "Hey what's up," he greeted her when he answered. He hadn't heard anything from her since they had had sex and he was happy she called.

"Hey Bryce, I need you to meet me at The Phoenix. I got something you need to see." She spoke quickly into the phone, trying to sound as normal as possible.

"Right now?" Bryce asked.

"Yes, right now," she said before Omar snatched the phone away from her mouth and hung it up.

Bryce wasn't alarmed by the phone call; Mia had placed calls like that plenty of times. They usually ended with him meeting her in a secret place for a sexual episode. After yesterday he was definitely ready for another round. He wasted no time getting up and getting dressed.

Omar tossed her phone on the couch, removed her restraints and forced her to her feet at gunpoint. He pushed her towards the door and grabbed her keys off the table.

* * *

Bryce walked up to the site. The gate that was normally locked was unlocked and slightly ajar. He spotted Mia's car, but as he looked around she was nowhere to be found. He stepped inside the gate and walked towards the building. The building was still just a shell with some floors still needing completion and no sides on the building; allowing anyone to see through the entire structure except for plastic hanging everywhere. Strings of construction lights hung from makeshift ceilings enabling sight in the dark building in the middle of the night.

Bryce opened the gate of the elevator and called out to Mia and waited for a response. When she replied he followed the sound of her voice in order to locate her. Bryce walked through some pieces of white plastic hanging from the ceiling. When he reached the other side he was shocked by the sight of a battered Mia tied to a chair in the middle of the room.

"Mia!" Bryce yelled out while racing over to her, only to be stopped dead in his tracks when Omar stepped out of the shadows pointing a gun at him.

"Ah-Ah-Uh," Omar said. "Not so fast my friend," Omar playfully instructed.

Bryce was at a loss for words, he couldn't understand what was going on. Why was Mia's new boyfriend holding her hostage and him at gunpoint? Bryce thought to himself how things had just gone from bad to worse.

"What the fuck is going on Christion? What's this shit about?" he asked trying to get some clarity on the situation.

"You tell me; this is all your doing— at least that's what it'll seem like," Omar laughed.

"Christion man, you trippin' bruh," Bryce declared. He began looking around the room looking for a way to free Mia without getting them both killed.

"Bryce be careful. He killed Marcus and Erica and he raped Kim," Mia shouted.

"What?" Bryce said even more confused now.

"He's not who you think he is," Mia continued.

"Damn do you ever shut up?" Omar said striking Mia in the face with the butt of the gun. "My name isn't Christion. My name is Omar...Omar Hill. Sound familiar to you Bryce?" he asked.

Mia watched as Bryce face went from scared and confused to disbelief. The name hit Bryce's ears and bounced around in his head, conjuring up memories he had long buried hoping never to revisit them again. That name brought back thoughts of one of his biggest regrets he had in life. He spent most of his life trying to forget it.

"Yeah I think Bryce knows exactly who I am," Omar said walking behind Mia and grabbing her by the hair then pressing his gun to her head. "Tell her Bryce, tell her who I am," he dared.

Bryce stood frozen unable to speak. His biggest fear was

coming to life right before his eyes. The thing he had been hiding from Mia and the entire world was on the verge of being exposed. It was the reason he had nightmares at night. It was the reason he couldn't marry the woman that he loved so much. He wanted to tell Mia for so long but just couldn't find the words to tell her. Most times he just couldn't bring himself to tell her. After so many years of lying it had become second nature, he almost convinced himself. He was not the man everyone thought he was, he was a fraud. Standing there at the doorstep of the truth, he still couldn't bring himself to speak it.

"You see Mia, I'm not the only one that has been lying about who I really am," he said turning her head to look at Bryce. The look on Mia's face made Bryce look away from her ashamed to face her as the real him. "Open your mouth bitch!" Omar said shoving his gun in her mouth. "Look Bryce you either tell her or I'm gonna blow her fucking head off."

"You gonna kill us anyway Omar," Bryce replied finally able to speak seeing the gun in her mouth and the seriously deranged look in his eyes.

"Yeah you're right," Omar said cracking himself up. "But you should at least let her know why she is gonna to die. Tell her why I'm doing this to you," he demanded.

CHAPTER TWENTY-THREE

Bryce looked out the window one last time at the beautiful blue water just as the sun began to disappear and thought to himself how life couldn't be much better than it was at this very moment, then he leaned his seat back and gave into his heavy eyelids. He had only been sleep for what felt like 20 minutes or so when he heard a loud noise that shook the plane and woke him. He could smell something burning and when he opened his eyes he could see smoke slowly beginning to fill the cabin of the plane. His mother began to panic and he could see all those fears Tremaine had about flying instantly return. His father remained calm as he got up out his seat and walked to the cockpit to see exactly what was going on.

Bryce could hear the pilot tell his father that there was a problem; one of the plane's engines had caught on fire and they needed to land immediately. Over the Atlantic with no land in sight, their plane was now freefalling fast. Mr. Edwards returned to his seat and yelled for everyone to buckle their safety belts and brace themselves for impact.

Bryce watched as Tremaine struggled with his safety belt. The nervous energy was getting the best of him, he couldn't seem to get it to close and lock. Mrs. Edwards began praying aloud, asking God to protect everyone on the plane, and if it was in his will for them to die than she asked that he would welcome them into his kingdom.

Bryce, still noticing Tremaine's troubles, decided to speak up. "Dad, something is wrong with Tre's seatbelt, it won't fasten!" he shouted at the top of his lungs.

Mr. Edwards unlatched his safety belt and raced over to help Tremaine. He messed with the belt until he finally got it locked. "Everything is gonna be okay, alright Tre?" he said seeing the fear on the young boy's face. "We gonna make it through this. I love you," he said rubbing the boy on the top of his head.

Tremaine didn't know what to say back. He was caught off guard by the affection from Mr. Edwards. He was only able to offer back an "okay" before the plane shook violently sending Mr. Edwards flying, slamming his head up against the door to the cockpit leaving him dazed.

Mrs. Edwards screamed at the sight of her husband being flung like a ragdoll. She tried franticly to get out her seat and aid him, just as she was able to get up out her seat the plane crashed into the water.

BOOM!

The front of the plane exploded on impact killing the pilot instantly. The fire blew the door off the cockpit sending it flying through the cabin hitting Mrs. Edwards in the head killing her immediately. Bryce screamed in agony at the sight of his mother being killed in front of him. As water begin filling what was left of the plane, Mr.Edwards was washed out into the ocean with a strong current. Both boys screamed and yelled for him as they realized they were left alone in the quickly sinking wreckage.

Tremaine's survival instincts kicked in first as he freed himself and made his way over to help his friend do the same. Bryce's safety belt was stuck and wouldn't open. Tremaine tried and tried to release him but he couldn't. Thinking fast as water was now up to his chest and almost covering Bryce while still seated; Tremaine instructed him to try and lift his feet up and stand up out the seatbelt. Bryce wiggled around trying to loosen the belt enough for him to do just that, but time wasn't in their favor with water flooding the plane.

"Tre don't leave me!" a frightened Bryce said.

"I'm not, just keep wigglin'." Tremaine reassured him.

"I got it," Bryce exclaimed as he now had enough room to stand up.

"Ok, c'mon," Tremaine said as the water was now almost above their heads. Tremaine turned and began swimming out of *the wreckage into the pitch black water. He finally reached the surface and was able to take a deep breath. After a few seconds he realized that Bryce hadn't come up and started to get nervous. He went back under the water, but quickly returned to the top as he realized he was unable to see anything, with fire burning all around him and smoke everywhere. He called out for his friend. "Bryce! Bryce! Bryce!" But he received no response.*

The water was freezing cold and he knew he wouldn't be able to last long in it. He spotted a piece of the wreckage, what appeared to be the wing, floating by and climbed up on to it and out of the frigid water. He laid on his back floating. He noticed something in the water next to him; it was the backpack with Bryce's name stitched on it. The one he had been holding with all his CDs in it. He reached into the water and grabbed it putting it against his chest and laying back on the floating piece of wreckage. Tremaine cried for hours thinking about losing the few people in the world who had truly cared about him. He cried and cried until he fell asleep somewhere in the middle of the ocean.

The sound of the helicopter hovering above him woke him up, but he was too weak to open his eyes. He could hear someone speaking to him over a bullhorn but couldn't make out what was being said. Next thing he knew he was being lifted up in the air and pulled into the rescue chopper.

"Are you okay?"

"Is there anything hurting on you son?"

"What is your name?"

Tremaine too weak to answer just laid there happy to be alive but sad at the fate of the Edwards family. One of the rescuers looked on the backpack Tremaine had clutched in his hand and looked over towards the other men and said, "This is Bryce, we found Bryce Edwards."

CHAPTER TWENTY-FOUR

"What?" a confused Mia said staring at the man she had known as Bryce for so many years. Thoughts flooded her head as she retraced all the time she had spent with him. She tried remembering if he had ever hinted or shown her anything to believe that he wasn't who he said he was. Mia thought of Bryce or Tremaine or whoever he was, saying that he wasn't ready to get married because he wasn't able to give 100% of himself to her. She had always felt like he was hiding something. Something that as of late he had seemed like he wanted to tell her but never got around to it. All his nightmares, him saying he felt guilty being alive all made sense to her. She wasn't even mad at him, she felt sorry for him. She had known his life story through the talks they had. She thought it was Bryce speaking to her about Tremaine's tragic past, but it really was him telling his own story.

"Yeah Mia, you sure know how to pick em," Omar quipped.

"So now what?" Tremaine asked looking at Omar with his gun in Mia's mouth. "Won't you just let her go. She has nothing to do with this. This is between me and you."

Omar removed the gun from her mouth, then grabbed Mia face, sticking his tongue down her throat kissing her. "Damn I'm gonna miss that," he said wiping the blood off her mouth and licking his fingers.

"I don't understand," Mia said still uncertain what was going on. "So what does that have to do with you Christion or Omar, whoever the fuck you are?"

"You want me to tell her?" Omar asked looking at Tremaine.

"He's my brother," Tremaine reluctantly said. "He's my lil' brother."

"Little brother?" Mia said in shock.

"Yup," Omar said. "The same little brother who thought you was dead for all these years. That was until I saw you on the news." He informed his brother.

"How'd you know it was me? After all these years?" Tremaine asked.

"I could never forget your face. You were all I had in this

world for so long. I looked up to you, wanted to be just like you. You were the coolest big brother. You taught me how to tie my shoes, my colors, how to play jacks, everything. When they said you died, I cried every day for a month," Omar explained and for the first time showed some emotion other than anger.

"I-I'm sorry I..." Tremaine tried to offer his sincerest apology, but Omar just ignored him.

"Do you know what I've been through in my life? Mom got clean and they let her get me back. We moved to New York and it didn't take no time for her to get back to her old ways, but she was worse this time," he explained to his brother. "The beatings got worse, her addiction got worse. She had me stealing, robbing and doing whatever to get her high. She sold me to a drug dealer for drugs Tre."

Tremaine stared at his brother pacing back and forth. He could see the hurt on his face which only made him feel guiltier. "I'm sorry O, I didn't know..."

"Nah, you didn't care," Omar said quickly shifting back into his angry state. "You didn't even come looking for me son. You just went about your life like I didn't exist. You had all this new money, this whole new life and you never tried once to find out what happened to your real brother. You a piece of shit nigga," he said aiming his gun at his brother. "You didn't even recognize me standing in your face," he said causing Tremaine to lower his head in shame. "You only care about yourself…oh and Mia," he said slowly turning the gun on her.

"Omar you ain't got to do this man," Tremaine tried to convincing him. "Just let her go, then me and you can figure all of this out."

"I look stupid to you?" Omar asked. "This shit only ends one way," he said with his finger now firmly on the trigger ready to squeeze.

Tremaine seeing no other option rushed him and tackled him causing the gun to go off. As the two brothers hit the floor the gun fell out of Omar's hand and slid out of his reach. Tremaine landed a right hook to his brother's jaw as they wrestled on the floor.

"Yeah you still my lil' brother," Tremaine grunted.

"Yeah but you hit like a bitch," Omar said landing a punch to Tremaine's stomach and another to his jaw dazing him. Omar jumped to his feet and began kicking his brother in the stomach and then in the head.

He walked over and picked up the gun then stood back over top of his brother. "Nigga fuck all this playin', change of plan," he said cocking the gun and aiming it at Tremaine lying on the floor. "Fuck you Tre."

BANG! BANG!

Omar stood looking down at Tremaine before dropping to his knees and collapsing on top of his brother, dead.

Tremaine looked up seeing Detective Hirsch holding

his gun. Bryce had a funny feeling about Mia's call and decided to use the card the detective had given him weeks earlier.

"Is everybody okay?" the detective asked.

"Yeah, I'm good," Tremaine said.

"Not me," Mia said from the tipped over chair she was still tied to.

Tremaine raced over to her ,untying her and rolling her over to see her bleeding from her shoulder, a result of being hit by the bullet Omar had fired meant for her head.

"It's just a flesh wound," said the detective. "Let me call it in," he said reaching for his police walkie.

BANG!

Mia screamed as Hirsch's head exploded and blood splattered all over Tremaine. Detective Jones stood over his dead partner with a smirk on his face.

"I never liked ya old ass anyway," he quipped.

"Yo what the fuck are you doing?" a shocked Tremaine stated.

"I knew you wasn't no good, you muthafucka," Jones said.

"Me? You just shot ya partner," Tremaine said.

"Nah, you did. Nobody will believe you didn't, you're not even who you say you are. How you think that's gonna look?"

Tremaine shook his head not believing the shit he was

hearing. He thought it was all over with Omar lying dead on the floor, but here he was right back in the same position.

"I hate you rich muthafuckas. I told you I would get you and now I got ya ass. You and that muthafucka over there were brothers working together. Yall killed Marcus, Erica, Hirsch and Mia…"

BANG!

Tremaine ducked hearing the shot ring out so close to him. He looked up to see a bloody Mia holding Hirsch's gun and Jones laid out on the floor dead. Mia collapsed into Tremaine's arms in pain.

"I love you Mia Armstrong," Tremaine said as he held her in his arms, happy she had saved their lives.

CHAPTER TWENTY-FIVE

2 Months Later

The beautiful water and white sand beaches of the resort in Provo, Turks and Caicos were doing their job of providing the rest and relaxation Tre and Mia were seeking when they decided to vacation there. The past 10 months had been so turbulent for the couple, but everything they had been through only strengthened their bond and love for one another, evident by the 10 karat diamond ring Mia was sporting around. Life was finally getting back to normal. Tremaine was back running Edwards Development Inc as its rightful heir, after Mia discovered paperwork showing

The Edwards had formally adopted Tremaine before the plane crash. Tre realized that was the surprise Mr. Edwards had been keeping from the two boys during their trip. He was riding high after the long awaited opening of The Phoenix had been a huge success. Mia too had much to celebrate: her best friend Kim had made a full recovery and was out the hospital and career wise, she chose to turn down the offer to become partner at the firm, instead deciding to open her own firm.

Tre watched from a table of the beachfront restaurant as Mia walked off the beach wearing a sexy white two piece swimsuit, tying her wrap around her waist, taking a seat joining him at the table.

"So, you enjoyin' ya self?" Tre asked the beauty.

"Hmm- mmm," Mia said while chewing the cocktail shrimp she had swiped off his plate. "Why you didn't order me some?" she said after swallowing the delicious appetizer.

"I got you," he charmingly said smiling at her.

"Ooh I gotta pee," Mia said trying to whisper. "I'll be right back," she said standing up from the table grabbing her bag off the table and kissing him.

Tremaine sat looking over the menu waiting for Mia to return, trying to decide what to order.

"You should try the oxtails, they're pretty good here," a voice said.

Tremaine looked up from the menu seeing the familiar

face of the brown skinned, athletic built man with a goatee and his dreads pulled back, wearing a white wife beater and khaki cargo shorts sitting across from him. "Not like Trina's," he said with a smile.

"Nah, nothing messin' wit Trina's," Bryce said sticking his hand out dapping his best friend.

The two men had been meeting for years at different location throughout the world. Bryce had been rescued by a group of fishermen after floating on a piece of debris like Tremaine. He was raised by a family in the Bahamas, under the name Fabian Anderson. The two reconnected while Tremaine was in college. Bryce expressed to Tre that he was happy being a normal kid with a normal life and wanted no parts of being Bryce Edwards. The two grown men still favored each other but not as much as they once had as children. But they were still as close.

"So you still think being rich is all it's cracked up to be, Tre?" Bryce asked referring to the talk they once had as eleven year olds.

"Hell no," Tremaine said leaning back in his seat. "This shit crazy," he admitted shaking his head.

* * *

Mia paced back and forth in front of the stall in the empty bathroom. She hadn't been feeling like herself as of late, but she hadn't paid it any mind until she missed her period. Her cycle had never been off and in her mind she already knew what she was waiting for the pregnancy test she had just taken to confirm. The thing she wasn't sure of was who it was she was pregnant by, Tre or Omar. After a few minutes Mia stepped back in the stall to see the results of the test. "Two lines," she said to herself.

Mia could see Tre sitting at the table talking to someone. He was smiling and laughing with the unknown man. She couldn't really get a good look at him because his back was to her. She approached the two men going unnoticed due to the laugh they were sharing. The closer she got she realized she had never seen the man Tre was talking to but by the way they were talking they definitely knew each other.

"Exactly, that's what I was talkin about," Tremaine said laughing harder.

"Who's your friend Tre?" Mia inquired catching the two men off guard as they both stared up at her with blank looks on their faces.

THE END.

EAT, PREY & NO LOVE

ABOUT THE AUTHOR

Raised in Peekskill, NY, Ty Marshall is an undeniable talent with a highly skilled pen. Discovered by New York Times Selling Authors Ashley & JaQuavis, his ability to seamlessly weave authentic depictions of the street with great storytelling sets him apart from the pack. He is widely considered one of the rising African American authors in the country. Ty has independently released several titles which include: Keys to the Kingdom, 80's Baby and Eat, Prey & No Love. He also released a ebook through St. Martins Griffin entitled Luxury & Larceny. Ty is a proud husband and father that currently resides in Atlanta, Ga.

www.TYMARSHALLBOOKS.com

www.ingramcontent.com/pod-product-compliance
Lightning Source LLC
Chambersburg PA
CBHW050030180626
46810CB00002B/655